PRAISE FOR
A HEAVEN OF THEIR CHOOSING

"Reading *A Heaven of Their Choosing* is like touring a set of rooms inside the enormous house of fiction. At the center of each sits a character, often isolated and regretful, whose interior is revealed with a candor and dead-pan irony reminiscent of the stories of John McGahern and even Joyce. Like them, Smith knows how to invade people's privacy while keeping a steady eye on the everyday world around them. And sometimes, lives defined by boredom and limitation are lifted by event into insight and wonder. She is a writerly writer, whose stories will appeal to readers who wish to experience not just what happens next but how, sentence by sentence, it manages to happen at all."
—**Billy Collins, Poet Laureate of the United States from 2001-3**

"Joann Smith's *A Heaven of Their Choosing* is a collection of authentic, gut wrenching, raw, hold-your-breath, can't-put-them-down stories. There is a miracle in these pages that transports the reader to the place where art transcends us, a place where it is possible to simultaneously feel pain and pleasure, joy and sorrow, and reach an epiphany: there is hope for us all. It is a collection one will return to again and again and again. "
—**Patricia Dunn, author of *Last Stop on the 6***

"I was riveted by *A Heaven of Their Choosing*. With a flair for mesmerizing irony inside of unerring truths, Smith delves into the power of language in our lives. From a wife's correspondence hidden in a honeymoon suitcase to a young employee at a gun shop's curiosity about a customer's choice of target, Smith delivers a collection of exquisite stories that will make you look at yourself and the choices in your life anew."
—**Jimin Han, author of *A Small Revolution***

A HEAVEN OF THEIR CHOOSING

stories by

Joann Smith

7.13 Books
Brooklyn

Printed in the United States of America

First Edition
1 2 3 4 5 6 7 8 9

These stories appeared in the following journals: "Something Grand," *Adelaide Literary Journal,* "Phlebotomist's Day," *Two Hawks Quarterly* "A Prayer at the Sandbar," *Whitefish Review,* "Purge," *Emerald Coast Review,* "Heavenly," *The Examined Life Journal,* "Tuesday Night at the Shop and Shoot," *Chagrin River Review* and was anthologized in *Lock and Load: Armed Fiction,* "You're Still Here," *Clockhouse Journal,* "Taking Notes," Servinghouse Journal, "A Matter of Faith," *New York Stories.*

Cover art by Olivia Croom Hammerman
Edited by Leland Cheuk

Library of Congress Cataloging-in-Publication Data

ISBN (paperback): 978-1-7361767-4-0
ISBN (eBook): 978-1-7361767-5-7
LCCN: 2020953037

A PRAYER AT THE SANDBAR | 1
YOU'RE STILL HERE | 5
SOMETHING GRAND | 21
PHLEBOTOMIST'S DAY | 35
GRAVESTONES | 41
A MATTER OF FAITH | 51
SEAMUS | 63
PURGE | 71
WALL MAN | 77
HEAVENLY | 87
SEEKING GRACE | 99
A HEAVEN OF THEIR CHOOSING | 117
TUESDAY NIGHT AT THE STOP AND SHOOT | 131
TAKING NOTES | 143

This book is dedicated to my husband, Bob, and my daughter, Mia, for their support and inspiration.

A PRAYER AT THE SANDBAR

No one says anything to the three women who have taken off their bikini tops, though people look at them with interest, with disapproval. They sit in size order—DD, C, B+/A-. I find the smallest most appealing because of the way they poke out so cheerfully, defying gravity, unlike the other women's.

The women are trying hard to be nonchalant, as if they've done this at every beach they've been to, as if they made a promise to do this and as awkward as it feels, they're seeing it through. I'm a regular here at this little bay; I've never seen them before. It's a family beach but without the dozens of kids—more paunches than sandcastle builders. No lifeguard, no bathrooms, no concessions, no garbage cans. It's a place where, when the tide is out, you can walk at least half a mile and still not be in water over your waist. I learned that years ago when my daughter and her friend, both eight years old, drifted out on their blow-up boat. Far out. I was collecting jingles— the delicate creamsicle-colored shells that my daughter and I first discovered on this beach, fell in love with, and decided to collect for a vase we were planning to fill. I was cultivating independence— hers from me and mine from her, and so was glancing up periodically, resisting the urge to curtail her adventure. But as happens with me when I'm by water, I eventually lost track. Water can do that to me—erase the world around me and all my connections. I had checked on the girls a moment before, but when I checked again, they were growing smaller in the distance. It took me almost ten minutes—which is a long time when you're trying to get to your only child—of walking, jogging, paddling through the water to get to them. Her friend had no idea they might be in danger because her back was to the beach. But my daughter, who was facing the other way, knew how far from me she had drifted. She started waving as soon as she saw me coming and kept waving as though I might lose track again. She cried when I got to her—sorry, relieved, terrified.

"You have to pay attention when you're in the water. You're far out."

She knew that; she knew they should have turned back. "I didn't know how."

I, too, was sorry, relieved and terrified. I wanted to make my negligence seem not as bad as it was. "But look," I said, waist-deep, "You can stand here."

She rolled out of the boat, rolling her friend out, too, laughed, hugged me, asked me to give them a ride back to shore. I should have made her do it—a lesson in rescuing herself.

"Get in," I said. Because whose fault was it really?

Anyway, no one says anything to the topless women. People try not to look, or try not to be seen looking. It's the Hamptons, but it's not that Hamptons. You have landed on the wrong beach, ladies. I keep sneaking a peek at the smaller woman . . . because I am/was small-breasted. Mine are fake now, so I don't consider myself as having a size. But when I had real ones, I resented their smallness. Now, I think of them fondly. Of the three women, if I could have a choice of their breasts, I'd pick the small ones.

What if I took *my* top off? Or rather, took my long-sleeved sun shirt off, then peeled my one-piece bathing suit down—cups facing out—and sat in my chair with my saline implants, tattooed nipples, and scars on view. Oh, how political. What a feminist. An activist. A survivor. A warrior. The women would smile at me, probably come over and embrace me, breasts to fake breasts. Hear me roar.

Instead I go into the water and forget them. "Hello bay." I float on my back and look into the sky.

By the time I get out, the topless women are gone and the tide is going out, exposing the sandbar. I walk out to it as I do almost every evening. But today, I want more from it than the shells, the rocks, the eddies full of minnows and the clams, not so deep in the muck, that it offers. This is the place where my daughter and I found a giant conch three years in a row—at least six inches long—with a huge snail inside, whose foot we tickled so it curled like a thick tongue. We called him Sheldon, put him back. Found him again the next year and the next. (Maybe not Sheldon, but we decided to believe it was.) I lie in the wet sand, wanting to dissolve into the bay instead of going home to my soup (though it is clam chowder, homemade in the deli).

At first I feel like something the bay sneezed up—slimy with the wet sand and weeds, slick like the rocks and shells. But then I settle into it. The wet sand world, different from the wet water world. Not the buoyancy of my body in water but the weight of it, gathering on the bulge of sand, settling downward. A sigh. All the tiny waves hitting me—I'm the Gulliver of this island—are sighs.

What would it feel like to close my eyes? Oh. The exhale of the bay against my body. The breath of the breeze. The sand doesn't have texture anymore; it's just a yielding support, accepting me, taking me. If I believed in magical realism, this is where I'd become Sheldon, or a water weed. This is when my backbone would start to dissolve into sand. It is almost sleep. I hardly recognize it. It eludes me in my bed, on my couch. Only on my deck can I sleep. Late at night there are no bugs, or few. But there are night animals. I've been sniffed.

The sun is low in the west. And now the bay is sighing from the other direction; the sand under me is shifting, dispersing. Tide is coming in.

"Hello again. Here I am again. Sky of God. Here I am lying

on a sandbar, still wanting and needing but feeling that I can't ask because I have so much, and so many have so little. So, I'm just here saying hi, knowing that you know what I want, so I won't ask. I'll just say "Hi." And, "You know." And then just a whisper because there are so many prayers and maybe you've forgotten mine . . . "Don't let the cancer come back." And then I want to ask for more, so much more.

I have to pee, and then it feels like I'm lying in my own piss, so I lift my hips and rinse my suit. There. But my needing and wanting and peeing have broken the spell and I'm wondering why no one is coming out to see why I'm lying on the sandbar. Why is no one concerned? True, there is no one on the beach, but there are people in the little cottages that front the bay. But that's just more wanting—wanting someone to come find me.

"Goodbye bay. Goodbye sky. Goodbye God."

Like sex (I do remember it), the after is wet and sticky. But I have a towel to sit on in my car and shampoo and conditioner at home for my stiffening hair.

The moths are soon throwing themselves against the screens. Night comes a little earlier now.

With a towel around me and my hair soaking in the leave-in conditioner, I pour my chowder into a pot, pour a glass of wine. I have crusty bread, too. Not so bad. Not so lonely.

And look, a message on my phone from my daughter. Grown and with a daughter of her own. She wants to come. To bring her baby girl to the bay "where we collected the orange shells. What were they called? And to the sandbar. Remember Sheldon? Maybe we can find daughter of Sheldon or granddaughter. Anyway, I want to come before the summer ends."

This is really the thing I want more than all the other things, God and sky and bay. Give me this and you don't have to give me anything else. My baby, her baby, and me. At the bay. Thank you.

YOU'RE STILL HERE

I LIE IN BED listening to my daughter crying. In a minute, I'll get up and walk to her room and find her sleeping because the crying is in my head where it loops and loops.

I should sleep now when it's possible. But it's not really possible. I'm waiting for the real crying to start; it will sometime between midnight and 2 a.m. Night terrors that have been going on for almost a year.

When I can't wait any longer, when I know the crying is still in my head but I have to confirm it anyway, I go to her room and find her sleeping soundly on a horizontal in her toddler bed, her feet planted on the smudged coral wall that I've given up touching up with paint, her hair dangling in a perfect black crescent off the other end. I consider waking her because one of the websites on night terrors suggests disrupting the sleep cycle. But it's just too counter- intuitive—let sleeping babies lie. And tonight might be the night, finally, when she doesn't wake screaming.

But it isn't. I'm lying on her floor when the mumbling starts. Before I can get to my knees, the mumbling becomes whimper- ing, and by the time I'm kneeling by her bed, it has ratcheted up to wailing. There's no mistaking it for the drone in my head. She rises onto her hands and knees in the yoga pose known as cow, but her back is not merely stretching in an inverse arch; it is an impossible bowl, and her face strains upward as if she is trying to deliver herself to the ceiling, which, in her maniacal trance state, I could almost believe she could manage.

"Mama's here."

Her eyes are open, but they relay no information to her brain; I'm image without meaning.

"Mama's here."

She bucks at my touch, drops to the mattress and thrashes like a fish on a boat deck straining for its proper reality.

"Shh. Mama's here." I talk of myself in third person, *Mama* seeming so much more potent than *I*. But the magic of *Mama* fails in this nether world of neither sleep nor wakefulness that she is spirited away to every night. Still, I offer it again. "Mama's here."

She recoils, screeches. I have to move her; there are neighbors and a bedroom just on the other side of this wall that she batters now with her feet. The woman next door has complained, politely, but asked, suspiciously, "every night?" when I told her night terrors. "Every night," I answered, feeling guilty of something.

"Cassie-Li." She arches and head butts, kicks and then stiffens as I collect the chaos of her in my arms. I manage to get her up and into the living room, tumble her onto the couch, and make myself a barrier. She rolls; I roll her back. Then I make a quick pivot on my knees, grab the remote and click on the TV. "Look, TV," I try to distract her out of it. She keens. I get an arm under her, try to pull her into a hug because another website says that night terrors could be a sign of attachment disorder, and there is a therapy that recommends holding the child through her rampage, showing her that she will be held no matter what. She catches the bridge of my nose with her head and howls.

"Ouch." I lower her to the couch.

Now Michael gets up. "Damnit, I've got to get some sleep. Every fucking night with this." He pushes himself in at the couch and puts his face close to hers. "Cassie-Li," he scolds. "Cassie-Li, stop it." She flails, hitting him in the face. "Don't hit me. Do you hear? Don't hit me."

"Oh, that's good, Michael," I dig at him. "Discipline her now. That'll work."

"Shut up."

During these episodes, we say things to each other we would not say in the light of day. In the morning, we will apologize and hug and promise not to take it out on each other that night.

"You shut up," I answer.

Now, he tries to gather her in his arms. "She won't let you."

"We're supposed to hold her, aren't we? You said the website said to hold her."

"It's just a stupid website. I don't know if it's right."

She arches, wails. He insists, picks her up as she throws her upper body away from him. He gets her upright, pins her arms.

"You're holding her too tight."

He ignores me, walks with her, trying to hug the motion out of her. "Cassie-Li, it's Daddy." He, too, seeks power from third person. "Shh. Shh. It's okay." He hums. She frees an arm, waves it wildly, stiffens and shrieks.

"Give her to me," I say.

"This can't go on."

"Give her to me."

He turns her toward me. "Be careful."

In the transfer, she scratches my neck. "Mama's here. Shh. Mama's here." I walk back and forth across the small living room. "Shh. Let's go out on the terrace. Let's go see the stars. Okay? Shh."

"It's raining," Michael reminds me.

"Open the door for me."

He does. "I'll get her an ice pop." Sometimes the coldness against her lips brings her out of it.

When I step out onto the concrete floor, it's wet and cold on my bare feet. I murmur to her. "I wonder where the stars are? Oh, there's one," I point, and when she follows my finger, I know she's back. That's how it ends—with a blink or a yawn—quietly and all at once: she's not there, then she's there. Like a peekaboo game. "See it?" I hear the strain in my voice. "It's a cloudy, rainy night. And chilly. Brr." I cuddle her.

Her breaths quaver, and she points, "Star."

It isn't; it's a plane. "Yes." I watch the sky for a bit longer, shiver with my bare feet. "Let's go back inside," I suggest cautiously. She doesn't object, and so I bring her back in, sit down on the couch, and pat her tear-chapped face with the Chinese fan-patterned throw that someone gave us as a present when we adopted her.

"Hi, Cassie-Li. Hi, Dolly." Michael comes and hands her an orange pop, unnecessary now but an earned reward for all of us. Michael and I smile wanly at each other. Cassie-Li licks.

"It's baby bug's happy birthday." She reminds us of the game we were playing with her ladybug finger puppet earlier in the evening.

After a few sucks on her pop, her head begins to bob. I take the pop from her, hand it to Michael, lift her. "Let's go back to bed now," I whisper. She rests her head on my chest; her hair is soaked with perspiration and the moisture works its way through my T-shirt. Michael keeps a hand on her head, one on my back as he walks with me to her room. I lay her head on her pillow and pull the covers down all the way because another website suggests that there's a correlation between feet and the place in the brain where terrors originate, so feet should be free during sleep. I've cut out all the feet from her footie pajamas and turned them into hand puppets. Michael and I stand there for the few moments it takes for her breathing to fall into its sleep rhythm. So easy. So peaceful.

It's 1:40 a.m. when we go back to bed—a thirty-minute episode. Michael and I talk for a few minutes—neurologists, her abandonment, attachment disorder, exhaustion, exhaustion. He falls asleep before I do.

When she calls at 6:20 a.m., Michael is quick to get out of bed. I steal another ten minutes. When I do get up, he and Cassie-Li are on the floor playing with her plastic farm animals.

"Did she scratch you?" Michael asks as he gets up to shower. I touch the sting on my neck. "Call the pediatrician today."

"We've called him. We've seen him. He'll just say she'll outgrow it. He'll say to give her Benadryl. You know that doesn't work on her. It keeps her up."

"There's nothing wrong with calling and asking again."

On four hours sleep, almost all of our discussions become arguments, so I say, "Fine."

When he leaves for work, he says, "Try and nap."

And I say, "I don't know how you do it—going to work on so little sleep." They are the morsels of kindness we offer each other, reminders of our sanity, of our humanity, of our love for each other.

The letter of the day is S. I drift and drift again and wake to *Clifford the Big Red Dog* whose voice is still reassuringly that of John Ritter, even though he has died.

"Come up, Mommy," Cassie-Li implores as I begin to drift again. I surface, rouse myself, give her some Cheerios, manage to shower. It's after 11 a.m. by the time I get us both dressed and out.

When I'm sitting next to her in the bagel shop finishing off my second latte and finally coming fully awake, I decide, once again, that Cassie-Li doesn't need a neurologist, that the sleep problem will resolve itself, maybe even tonight, that she's a happy, attached child whose brain just hasn't learned yet how to pass smoothly from one sleep cycle to the next. She kneels, picking blueberries from her muffin and popping them into her mouth. She gives me a blueberry kiss.

"Delicious." I'm considering a third latte when she announces, "Pee-pee, mommy."

"Pee-pee? Are you sure?" I ask, hoping to dissuade her; I don't want to get up.

"Very, very pee-pee."

"Okay." I walk over to the woman behind the counter. "Do you have a bathroom?"

"Sorry."

"Mama, I can't hold myself." The only place on this block with a bathroom is a bar.

"Pew," Cassie-Li scrunches her face as we enter to the smell of sweetly acrid beer and dirty bar rags. But it's a familiar and still comforting smell to me. Bars were home for Tommy—my first love, my first husband—and me.

"Hi," I greet the bartender. "Can we use your bathroom? I just trained her." He nods.

In the bathroom, the seat is up and Cassie-Li palms the piss-stained rim before I can warn her not to touch anything.

On the way out, I catch myself singing softly, "Someone saved my life tonight, sugar bear," to the song on the jukebox as though it's so natural, as though it's the mid-seventies and Elton John should be playing on a jukebox, as though I'm still in my drinking days and I should take a stool at the bar with Tommy.

The bartender sees me singing and I say, embarrassed, "This song takes me back."

He smiles. "It's a time warp in here."

"Good song," says one of the three men at the bar, a regular by the looks of it. Tommy always made fun of me for the cheesy songs I liked. But he called me sugar bear.

I'm remembering the way Tommy and I would lift our shirts and sit chest to chest in my car because sometimes he just needed to feel me against him, and the way we made love on the pool table of Madden's Bar the night Hughie Madden let us sleep over there, and about how the bar was home so much more than my home was. And I'm remembering the sweetness of it because I'm feeling sentimental and because Tommy is dead—eleven years already—and because it was sweet, his calling me sugar bear; my leg hooked over his on our barstools; the way our friends surprised us with a wedding there one night, Hughie presiding, everyone dousing us with beer after the vows because, of course, no one had rice, and Hughie giving us the key to his apartment above the bar to consummate our marriage. And the cheers and jokes when we came back down an hour later. Then a real marriage a year and a half later and a divorce two years after that. I'm thinking that we were so young and wild and willing.

I kiss Cassie-Li on her head as I strap her into her car seat. Of course, there was the fighting, too, and Tommy's drinking that somewhere along the way slid into alcoholism, and our ugly, ugly breakup when I told him I hated him because I loved him so much but I couldn't keep on loving him. He laughed, saying it made no sense. And when I slapped him, he sent me flying across the room with one swipe of his hand. And then we held each other and sobbed. And it still takes my breath away, all of it, and I'm trying to recover, leave it behind again, as I push the car door closed and realize, too late, that my purse and keys are on the seat.

"Shit."

I pull on the door, check all the others—all locked. "Cassie, honey, can you open the door? Can you pull the button up?"

She smiles, sits forward but can't reach the button from her car seat. "Mama, come."

I look up and down the street as if a solution will present itself.

"Mama?" She flaps her fingers in a newly learned beckon.

I turn again and catch the eye of the regular who has been watching through the bar window. In a moment the door opens, and he comes towards me, squinting.

"Locked your keys in." He nods, proud of his assessment.

"Yeah." I look past him.

"I knew it," he says with great satisfaction. "I could tell by the look on your face. I said to myself, 'She locked her keys in there.'" He points back to the bar. "I was watching through the window, and I saw your face when you turned around, and I said, 'She locked her keys in the car.' Yup, I said it right out loud."

I continue to look past him, trying to make him realize that I have no use for him, that there will be no reward for what he clearly thinks is his amazingly astute observation.

He comes closer, peers into the car and taps the window.

"Don't do that. Please."

"You have the baby in there."

Another genius observation. "Excuse me." I position myself to block him from Cassie-Li's view, and in my proximity to him, I catch the boozy sweetness of his breath. Later it will have turned metallic and rancid.

"Chinese, right," he says, pointing to Cassie-Li and nodding. "Adopted?"

I have read article after article about how to respond to these stupid, insensitive summations and questions about her identity. She's more than Chinese; she's more than adopted. But also, she is Chinese; she is adopted. So, I don't always find the statements or questions as offensive as I'm supposed to.

"My niece has one."

Now I glare at him. Now I'm supposed to say, *Don't objectify her by saying "my niece has one" as though she's a thing.*

Then he adds, "She's gorgeous, just like your baby."

I slump. "I have to get her out of there."

"Do you have a spare set of keys?" he asks. "You'd probably use them if you did, right?" He chuckles.

Cassie-Li takes a finger from her mouth and drags it along the window. "Mama, come." But she's temporarily distracted by the shapes her salivaed finger makes.

"Can you call anyone?" he asks, refusing to let me ignore him. "Some kind of road service? Triple A? Not double A. You don't want double A," he says, smiling and looking to see if I've gotten the joke.

No double A. Tommy had mocked AA, too. Once when he stumbled off a curb, he said, "Quick, call double A, I need road service." It was funny at the time. Now, I don't smile. "My cell phone and all my numbers are in the car," I say, more to myself. "But I know my husband's number. I can call him. He could leave work, go home, and get the spare set." I'm calculating that that would take about an hour and a half.

The regular waves that idea away. "You don't want to bother your husband with this. Take my word for it." He says this as if he knows something personal about Michael and me.

"Can you go into the bar and call the police for me? I can't leave her."

"What? The police. Like Nine One One?" He shakes his head, sways. "No. I wouldn't do that. You never know with cops. They may think you left her in there and went to the store, or something. You know. . . went shopping. Or to the bar. That's the kind of thing people do. Not you. But people do it. You know who I mean. Then they take the baby from you."

This paranoia makes sense to me. I'm afraid that one night the woman next door will call the police, and the cops will come banging on my door to take my daughter away. So possible is this to me that when, about a week ago, Cassie-Li butted me in the lip with her head, and I bled onto her pajamas, I changed her into a clean set and threw the others out, right down the compactor chute so there'd be no evidence of anything the police might accuse me of.

"Shit." I'm considering breaking the window, and I spin in another 360-degree circle looking for something that can accomplish that. Cassie-Li—a child who never naps—is letting her eyes close. They say that the child doesn't remember the night terrors, and indeed, she awakens in the morning bright and cheerful as though from a long, pleasant sleep while Michael and I hunch with fatigue. Yet, she won't nap and doesn't fall asleep easily at night and never alone. She may not remember the terrors but some instinct tells her to fear sleep. So, it alarms me that she is falling asleep in the car. And though it's only been a few minutes, and it isn't more than seventy-three or seventy-four degrees, I imagine that she's cooking in there, losing oxygen and losing consciousness. Then my brain finally fires. "What about a locksmith? Isn't there a locksmith around here? Around the corner?"

"Sure." The regular leans into his heels, and I fear he'll keep going backwards but he tilts forward again.

"Can you go get him for me?"

"Yeah, he's around the corner. Around that corner." He points. "I know this neighborhood. I know all these places." He sweeps his arm. "Used to know. Everyone moved. Now it's all banks. How many banks do you need? Hmm? How much money do people have? This used to be a deli, this right here," he accuses the Apple Bank next to the bar. "Used to be able to get a nice sandwich there."

"Could you go get him for me? The locksmith? Or I can ask someone else." I look into the face of an elderly woman coming up the street.

"You think I can't find my way around the corner? I know my way around."

Drunken indignation. I recognize it. He pulls his cigarettes from his jacket pocket, taps one from the pack, finds his lighter, lights his cigarette and sucks on it, bends his head back and blows smoke rings. "You like that?" he asks, taking a step closer. "You like that?" he repeats more lasciviously.

This is familiar, too, the point at which the drunk thinks he is so desirable and so clever with double entendres.

I turn away and take a step in the direction of the bar where I will call the police—what I should have done in the first place.

"Wait." He exhales smoke. "Wait. I'm going. I came out here to help, didn't I?"

I ignore him and go into the bar. When I come out, the regular is gone. The police arrive quickly. I explain, blaming my exhaustion. One cop says, "Happens all the time." A slim jim is produced and the door is opened.

Cassie-Li snores quietly. I kiss her hair, which is soaked with sweat, and I roll down the window to cool her off.

As I'm pulling out, I see the regular listing up the block, a big man walking alongside, carrying a toolbox—the locksmith. The drunk's hands are going as he explains. I drive by. By the time I reach the corner, I'm crying.

"Daddy's home."

Michael comes through the door, and I go immediately to the couch. What I want desperately is a nap but like Cassie-Li, I don't nap. I've never been good at falling asleep, either.

Michael lies on the floor and lets Cassie-Li climb him—the mountain of daddy.

"Let's get the girl in to make dinner." He says it or I say it. Our little joke. The miraculous girl who will cook for us, put the food in front of us, clean up after us. It never gets old— this idea of the girl, no matter how many evenings it's been conjured. And we lie there conjuring her again and smiling. Later, at 1 a.m. we'll be sniping at each other. For now, the girl makes both of us happy.

"Let's order in," Michael suggests after the idea of the girl yields to the fact that one of us will have to get up and cook something. It's a lesser miracle but still a gift. He makes the call: meatball hero, eggplant parmesan hero, a salad—the eggplant and the salad are my attempts at getting vegetables into my body which I saturate everyday with caffeine and sugar. He says into the phone that he'll pick the order up.

To Cassie-Li, he says, "Baby dolly, do you want to come with daddy?" Every day he finds a new endearment to love her with. Doll doll. Honeybee. Honey doll. Sweet girl. He loves her so and hates that he loses his temper with her during the terrors.

When they're at the door, I shout, "Bring back ice cream, too." My sugar level has dropped off. Maybe later I'll tell him about locking Cassie-Li in the car. Maybe not.

I lie on the couch and let my mind go freely to Tommy. A few months before he died, he called and asked me to meet him in a bar. I had heard from him now and then after we split up. At first the calls were about us—did I think we'd get back together? Later, they became about slights to him—which baptism he wasn't invited to, who didn't say "thank you," when he said God bless you after someone sneezed. Towards the end, when the calls were rare and sometimes incoherent, he offered aggrandizements of small events he had participated in. He helped a woman carry her stroller down the steps of Grand Central Station. No one else helped. Only he. "It was amazing." Someone from high school materialized in a bar he was in and recognized him. "It was amazing."

"For old time's sake," he had said when he called. "Have a drink with me." I had heard he was drinking straight vodka by then out of a Poland Spring water bottle, squirting it into his mouth through one of those sport tops, thinking he was fooling everyone.

I drove to the bar that day and sat across the street in the parking lot of a bank, never deciding that I wouldn't go in but never moving from the car. I had left the chaos of our drinking behind; I always knew I would. Even when I married him, even as I said, "I do," I knew we couldn't last. Not so deep down, I wanted convention—sobriety, a family, a glass of red wine with dinner. I knew that at some point, I would look back on my drinking days with regret and sorrow—too bad I thought so little of myself/didn't have enough direction/wanted so badly to be a part of something that I spent so many nights in a bar. That I wanted to do more than spend our weekends in the bar once we were married, that I complained about his drunkenness, that I tried to change him, was, of course, a betrayal. So was my inability to conceive. He thought we were trying but I really wasn't. I called him a coward for not wanting to grow up and face life; he called me a coward for wanting to conform.

I sat in the car for three hours, then turned the key in the ignition and left.

Tommy died a few months later. He had lost his job and was living alone in a basement apartment. He was dead on the floor of his bathroom for at least a day before anyone found him. An embolism.

Cassie-Li doesn't want to go to bed. It's that vague something warning her against sleep. I sit on the loveseat in her room, tell her I'll stay until she falls asleep.

"Mama?" She checks every few minutes. "Mama?" She twitches awake.

"Shh. Mama's still here." She does it in the car, even though she can see me, at least the back of my head. "Mama?" As though at any moment, I could disappear. "Mama?" Plaintively.

After nearly thirty minutes, I say, "Cassie-Li, Mama's going to go out of the room now." She won't sleep, can't sleep as long as she has to check to see that I'm still there.

"No."

"Yes. Goodnight, now. I'll see you in the morning."

"No. Mama." I hug her, kiss her. She clings, cries. I peel her arms from my neck.

"Mama."

Michael and I have read two books on sleep. "She has to cry," he says authoritatively, as one of us does every night. And she does cry.

"I was thinking of going out." I say this all the time and never go.

"You should. She might go to sleep easier if you're not here."

So to him, it's my *refusal* to disappear that's the problem. He sees me translate his statement as blame; he sees me ready for the fight.

"I just mean that she has to know you have a life. You have to go out and come back. How will she know that you come back if you never leave?"

By the time I put lipstick on, find my shoes, take my jacket from the closet, Michael has repudiated all the authorities and is lying in her little bed with her.

I want to walk, but it's dark and women disappear in the dark. Tommy was right; I am a coward; I have become a coward, afraid of even taking an evening walk. I used to always walk when I got drunk. I'd get up from the bar and go and when I'd come back, he'd be furious. "You can't just disappear on me like that."

I don't want to be a coward, so I walk.

In another five hours Cassie-Li will be screaming, and I'll be agonizing over what she remembers. Her birth mother? The smell of her? The sound of her? The feel of the hard ground as this woman laid Cassie-Li down and walked away. The sudden and absolute aloneness? Disappearance? Is that her terror? Yes, I decide, remembering something from a website on attachment disorder. When Cassie-Li's birthmother laid her on the ground and disappeared, Cassie-Li disappeared, too, in a way. For fourteen days, (according to the orphanage records) Cassie-Li knew what it was to have a mother, to be a part of that mother, and when that mother walked away, Cassie-Li was too young to know of herself as an entity separate from that mother; her birth mother disappeared; Cassie-Li disappeared. So, when she checks, "Mama? Mama?" I wonder if it could be that it isn't only my disappearance she fears but hers, as well, that "Mama" goes out like echolocation—she finds me, she finds herself.

And maybe the regular worries about disappearing, too. Maybe he inserted himself into the story of my locked-in-the-car-keys because he needs to prove that he still exists, that he's still a part of the world. And Tommy, too. With his nothing stories about carrying strollers, maybe he was proving to himself that the world still existed, and he existed in it, that he hadn't disappeared, yet. Maybe he always knew how tenuous everything was and he drank to hold onto things. I thought of his drinking as a way of letting go, but maybe it was his way of holding on. And I should have gone into the bar that day when he asked me to because maybe he needed my help to prove to himself that he was still a part of things. And I should have waited for the regular to come back with the locksmith. I should have allowed him that importance. I will go back to the bar and say thank you. I will let him know that he mattered. But not now. Now I will walk back home.

I sit on the floor in her room waiting. Tonight, it won't be "Mama's here" that I try to soothe her with. The whimper comes early, just before midnight, then the muttering.

"Shh, Cassie-Li." I kneel at her bed and bring my mouth close to her ear just as she's beginning to stiffen. "Shh. You're here. You're still here."

SOMETHING GRAND

"My God, it's the church," Mary Ryan cried as she and her neighbors Dora Amato and Eddie and Carol Edmunds turned the corner onto the Grand Concourse.

Mary Ryan had been lying in bed when she heard the sirens nearing. She caressed Mike's side of the bed, just once, her hand wide and slow along the clean sheets. He died there the day before, lying down after dinner, saying he didn't feel well and suffering a heart attack, while Mary was in the kitchen cleaning the vegetable drawers of the refrigerator; she changed the sheets after coming back from the hospital that night, not wanting to get into a bed where a dead body had lain. When the smell of smoke wafted through her window, she got up and looked out, then dressed and went downstairs, as several of her neighbors had, in search of the fire.

Carol Edmunds pushed through the gathering crowd toward the police barricades, beckoning the other three to follow. A fireman in a cherry picker flooded the smoking roof with water, and the crowd gasped collectively when the flames shot through and he had to be reeled away. The three-quarters moon had settled above the church, and the black smoke off the tips of the flames twisted toward it. An exploding sound jolted Mary back onto the toes of a woman behind her: a stained-glass window blew out. A newspaper photographer took several shots of the gaping opening where the window had just burst then scanned the crowd for appropriately mournful faces. Carol Edmunds managed to get his attention. "I was baptized here," she told the photographer who was wearing an ID from *The Daily News.* "So were my husband and our three children." Mary Ryan said nothing. She had been baptized elsewhere in the Bronx, as had Mike and their daughter, Aileen. And though Mary had attended the 7 a.m. Mass at St. Philip's almost every day since they'd moved here twenty years ago and was in the church just that morning, and though Mike's funeral was supposed to have been held in the church two days from now, and he read *The Daily News* every day of his life, Mary would not pander for sympathy or attention. She discreetly patted the tears from her eyes.

Just your luck, she said now to Mike. He would have liked hearing that: he had spoken about his bad luck as if it were something romantic. But Mary had never allowed him his bad luck. "You have the same luck as everyone else," she told him over and over. "Disappointments, Mike, not bad luck. They're a part of life. Do you think you're some kind of privileged character who shouldn't have his share of disappointments?" She cringed now under the scathing of those words. He would have liked it so much better, been able to bear it all easier if he could blame it on bad luck—a trip over his own two feet that left him with a bad back; fired from his job at the insurance company because everyone else in his department was taking bribes to set the claims high, and he had not only never taken so much as a penny but was up for a promotion; not being left the money he was promised by a great aunt; not winning the 50-50 at Church. He could manage to smile about it when he considered it bad luck—the bad luck of having bad luck—as if it were almost charming. But Mary wouldn't let him have it. Why had she been so harsh? Why was it so important to her that he acknowledge disappointment? What would their marriage have been like if she had been able to say "poor Mike," and then take him in her arms, instead of telling him to stop feeling sorry for himself?

The photographer took a photo of Carol and moved on.

"Do you see this?" asked Father Ahearn, the pastor, coming over.

"It's awful," Carol answered, taking his hands in hers.

"Our beautiful church," he grieved. Then he gently pulled his hands from Mrs. Edmunds and reached for Mary. "How are you?"

Now she took his soft hands in hers. "I'm so sorry about this, Father."

He shook his head, turned to look at the burning building then back at Mary. "And Mike," he said. "Poor Mike. I'm afraid we can't have his funeral in the church now."

"No, I see that," Mary said, and they both regarded the stone steps down which a rush of water poured.

"But don't worry," Father Ahearn reassured her. "We'll set up the auditorium in the school for Masses. We can do the funeral in there if you like."

"You mean the gym?" Mary recalled the room that served as auditorium, dance hall, and basketball court.

"Or we can call one of the other churches."

Mary hesitated. "I just want him to have a nice funeral," she said. "He deserves that."

"If anyone deserves it, it's Mike," Father Ahearn affirmed. "I don't think anyone loved the church more than Mike did."

Mary nodded but a familiar resentment rose in her. She was the one who attended Mass every day, walking up the hill no matter the weather. But it was Mike whom everyone noticed because he made such a show of going on Sundays. In his blue wool suit in the winter, the seersucker in the warm weather, his face clean shaved and braced with aftershave, he'd attend the 9 a.m. Mass, locking his hands in prayer. After that, he'd join the choir for the 10 a.m. Mass; and later, for the 11 and 12 he'd usher and help with the collections, parading up and down that long aisle for all to see, greeting as many people as he could, lingering with the priests afterwards as though he wished Masses would go on all day.

"Maybe we should do it in the school." Father Ahearn interrupted Mary's silent condemnations of her husband. "I think Mike would want to be here in the parish."

"I think you're right," Mary agreed, and then she bowed her head and asked God and Mike to forgive her unkind thoughts.

But that night her mind wrapped back to the old resentments—his refusal to share the responsibilities of the household and his confidence that his charm made up for it; the attention he got at church; the attention he got from neighbors whenever he took Aileen to the park on Saturdays while Mary cleaned the apartment. Later Mary would hear about it: "Isn't he wonderful with her!" "What a good father." "Oh, how he loves her." No one praised Mary for the bathing of, feeding of, cooking for, dressing of Aileen. No one said, "Oh what a good mother you are." No one noticed when she took Aileen to the park.

The next morning, Mary put on her brown- and black-striped dress, combed her short grey hair—Mike had always wanted her to grow it: "I miss your curls," he used to say. But Mary didn't have the patience for the unruliness of it. She walked up the hill at 200th Street, the smoke still pungent on her coat and on the morning air. The church had stopped burning, but it was smoldering and three fire trucks remained out front. On the school door was taped the top of a cardboard box with the words MASSES IN GYM printed in black Magic Marker. Inside, an unlit standing candle and two statues that had been saved from the flames were arranged in a greeting in a corner. A cloth-covered, collapsible table, which was to serve as the altar was set up in front of the stage. Mary took a seat in one of the folding chairs, and realized, as she started to her knees that, of course, there were no kneelers. She sat with her hands folded in her lap, her head bowed, and was unable to pray.

She fell into a fantasy about her marriage, imagining herself answering Mike without the sharpness in her voice. She lingered at the dinner table, chatting, instead of rushing to get the dishes done and a load of laundry in, suggesting a few numbers for his lottery tickets instead of complaining about the waste of it. He was different, too. He brought home strawberry ice cream, her favorite. After dinner, he cleared the table, then put dishes away while she washed, and they talked the whole time, laughed, even. He carried the garbage downstairs without her having to harp about it, and then he poured them a drink, always going a little past the point where Mary said to stop. It seemed that it would have been so easy, all of it, and yet, she had managed none of it. She reminded herself that one of them had to take charge, one of them had to keep the apartment clean, get the bills paid on time. One of them had to say no to Aileen when she always wanted yes. And since he didn't want to do it, she did. Still, she couldn't stop wondering what it would have been like if she had let the vacuuming go once in a while. Or if she had said "yes" to a Saturday matinee, like she used to when they were first married, instead of insisting that she needed to bleach the tub grout or reorganize the kitchen cupboards. Maybe they could have gone to the Botanical Gardens to see the daffodils. They had done that several times early in their marriage and when Aileen was young. Mary would have liked to see the daffodils again. She wondered if all widows did this—went over their marriages as if they were stories they could rewrite.

Forcing her attention to Father Ahearn's homily, Mary heard him persuade them that the essence of the church was not gone; it could still be found among them, in them. It was an appropriate sermon, one Mary expected, and she thought ahead to what Father Ahearn would say at the funeral. Surely, he'd talk about how much Mike loved the church.

When he held up the Eucharist, announcing "The Body of Christ," Mary couldn't bear not to kneel before it and awkwardly pushed a chair away and lowered herself to the hard floor.

At home, Mary Ryan set out the tuna and macaroni salad she had made during the night when she couldn't sleep, and two plates, and waited for her daughter. She hoped Aileen would bring the children—Tara, with her chubby pink hands, and Daniel Michael, the baby, who would come to Mary now without crying. With them in the room, Mary and Aileen could speak without having to look at one another, and that might be helpful when Mary had to tell Aileen that her father's funeral would be held in the school auditorium.

Aileen had taken the news of her father's death badly, of course. She and Mike were so much closer than she and Mary were. Mary expected the anger. But she expected a little sympathy, too. Instead, she got accusations. "Cleaning a vegetable drawer while your husband was dying, while my father was dying? Do you care about anything besides a clean house?" And "Did it ever occur to you to go in and check on him? Or to call an ambulance when he said he didn't feel well? Don't you know the signs of heart attack? Everyone knows the signs of heart attack."

She told Aileen she couldn't have done anything. Mike always went to bed before Mary did. Should she have checked on him every night? And why would she call an ambulance when he only said, "I don't feel so well?" His back often bothered him; Mary assumed it was that. But the way Aileen put Mary's cleaning of a refrigerator drawer and Mike's dying right next to each other in a sentence made Mary question her behavior. Why *couldn't* she have peeked in on him? It was because she had grown so intolerant of his neediness and his lack of awareness that she might be needy, too, that she stopped giving him what he wanted most—her attention. How different would their lives have been if she had not begrudged him his neediness, if she had been able to see it as just a desire for love, a desire for her? How hard would it have been for her to peek in on him with a simple "How are you?" or "Would you like a glass of water?" How he would have appreciated that.

Just before noon, expecting Aileen on time, Mary went to the living room, took two photograph albums from the hutch and placed them on the kitchen table by Aileen's setting—an offering of some sort. While she waited, Mary flipped through the pages, recalling the circumstances of each photo. There were fewer, by far, of her and Aileen than of Mike and Aileen, and though that was only because Mary was better with the camera, and really didn't like to have her picture taken, it reminded her of how obviously Aileen preferred Mike's company and how much more of a history they had than Mary and Aileen had. And why not? Mike was the fun parent and Aileen had always been a daddy's girl.

"Where are the children?" Mary asked when she opened the door to her daughter at nearly 12:45.

"You don't bring children to a wake," Aileen explained impatiently. "Danny's watching them, and we have a sitter coming. He'll meet us at the funeral parlor later."

But no one ever said that Mary couldn't be a fun parent, too. And Mike had tried to cajole her, telling her to leave the laundry and join him and Aileen in the park or at the zoo. But she would answer him with *Who'll do it if I don't?* If memory served her correctly, he hadn't responded with *I'll do it*, but only with *It can wait.* How was she supposed to let it wait? How was she supposed to let them go without clean socks and underwear? Plus, she didn't know how to compete with Mike for Aileen's affection, and that's what it always felt like to her—a competition that she knew she would lose. So she accepted her role, and sometimes Aileen needed Mary's steadiness and practicality but more often she wanted Mike's lightheartedness.

Aileen didn't eat but picked up one of the albums and leaned at the sink while Mary worked the salad around in her dry mouth. She glanced over at Aileen's unused place setting on the table and understood all at once that from now on, she'd be eating alone, trying to swallow every night for the rest of her life.

"We should bring some of these to the wake," Aileen said, removing a photograph from its sleeve. "I want to put them out so people can remember him the way he was, not the way he'll look in the coffin."

Mary gave up on the salad.

Aileen took several other photos from the book and placed them on the table; only one included Mary. "I want them back,"

Mary said, getting up and scraping the remaining salad off her plate into the garbage. Aileen sat down, while Mary put her dish and the one Aileen didn't eat from, in the sink and began to wash them.

"Leave those for now," Aileen said.

"And who'll do them?" She immediately regretted the harshness of her habitual refrain and added more gently, "Look at your pictures. I'll be right there."

Aileen huffed then stated, "I'd like to keep some of these."

"I don't think I want you breaking up the albums. You can come and look at them whenever you want," Mary answered.

"I want to take them with me. I don't know when I'll be back."

Mary looked up at the wall and then back down to the sink. Aileen had visited once or twice a month, but with Mike gone, she wouldn't be making that kind of effort.

"Remember his harmonica?" Aileen went on pretending not to know that she'd just given Mary an emotional body blow. "Does he still have that?"

"He never played it."

"He's playing it right here in this photo. He played it for me."

Mary took that blow, too. "Did he? How nice."

"I think he used to keep it in his top drawer. Can I go look?" Aileen got up before Mary answered.

Mary finished the dishes and walked to the bedroom behind her daughter, then stood next to her as Aileen slowly pulled open the top drawer, and the smell of Mike escaped.

"His Sunday smell," Aileen whispered.

"Yes, his aftershave," Mary said. "It's like he just walked through the room."

Aileen picked up and regarded the various items in the drawer that Mary knew by heart: his wallet, from which she had already removed thirteen dollars; the broken-handled coffee cup that held his pennies; papers that Mary had gone through; his cufflinks and tie clip; a medal of St. Joseph that he never put on a chain; palm from last year's Palm Sunday service; the harmonica; a deck of cards and his Old Spice.

"Here it is," Aileen said, taking up the harmonica. She blew through it barely making a sound. I'd like to put this out at the wake, too. I like the idea of having something personal there, something that was special to him."

Mary didn't see the point, but she didn't argue. "Just make sure I get it back."

"I'd like to keep this, too," Aileen answered. "I might teach myself to play."

"Fine. You think about what you'd like, and we'll discuss it. But I don't want you ransacking your father's drawer now."

"I'm not ransacking. I want a few of his things. What do you care about the harmonica, anyway? You didn't even know he played it. You'll probably just throw everything out."

Mary wanted Aileen to know that she wished she could have done things differently, better. But she couldn't say that without crying, and she didn't think Aileen wanted to see her cry; she wouldn't have believed that Mary's tears were sincere.

"Take whatever you want," Mary said.

"The photos and the harmonica. And maybe that holy medal."

Mary nodded. "His St. Joseph. I bought it for him when you were born. He loved being a father. St. Joseph was his favorite saint—the father of Jesus. You *should* have that."

Aileen took the items she wanted, and then said she needed to put on some makeup for the wake and went into the bathroom.

Mary stood looking into the open drawer after her daughter left the room. She decided she'd keep everything just as it was. She knew Aileen was right and she could be unsentimental, and in the right or wrong mood throw just about everything out. She picked up Mike's wallet and took the time to examine the items in the pocket behind the credit card sleeve. She found a card identifying him as Catholic and requesting that a priest be called in case of emergency; a card stating his O+ blood type; his lottery tickets (wouldn't that really just be Mike's luck); a faded, folded rectangle of construction paper on which Aileen had written "All All My Love." It was a Christmas present. Aileen had given each of them one when she was six years old, though Mary's message only contained one "All." Aileen had wanted her father to know she loved him more. Mary still had hers in the bottom of her jewelry box. She took Mike's out deciding to give it to Aileen. Then she pinched out a small, blue velvet pouch; she recognized it right away—the case he kept his caul in. He was born in "a sack," he used to say, a membrane covered his entire body. The doctors told his mother it was a very rare occurrence and they carefully cut it, dried it, and gave it to her in that pouch. His mother told Mike about his unusual birth when he was a child, convincing him that the caul made him very special, very lucky. Mary had enjoyed the story when she first heard it but grew tired and even disgusted by it in the many retellings. She had no idea that he kept the caul with him; if she had, she probably would have told him to throw it out, that it was a ghastly thing to carry around. But now she was suddenly teary at the thought that he carried the caul believing that at some point, the good luck it was supposed to bring would finally kick in. *But you had good luck, Mike Ryan*, she whispered to him. *Everyone loved you.* Mary put the wallet back in the drawer, went out to the kitchen, and put the pouch and the love note in her purse.

In Aileen's car on the way to the wake, Mary informed her of the fire. "Then where's the funeral?" Aileen asked.

"In the auditorium."

"The gym?" she asked, incredulous. "Couldn't you have gotten another church?"

Mary said she couldn't, keeping Father Ahearn's offer to herself, promising Aileen that they had done up the room nicely, respectfully, reminding her of how her father loved the parish, how he would have wanted the funeral there.

"He loved the *church*," Aileen corrected her.

Aileen parked and rushed to get out of the car, away from Mary.

"Wait. I found this in his wallet." Mary extended the love present.

"He kept it." Aileen pressed it to her chest, kissed it, and then put it in her purse.

Mary didn't tell her that she had kept hers, too.

During the wake, people did glance at Aileen's photographs and the harmonica that she laid out next to them, but for the most part, they talked about the fire. Danny came, as did his parents. Mary watched him find Aileen, watched the way she led him to the casket, the two of them kneeling together, shoulder to shoulder, their faces pointed towards Mike's. Early in her marriage, Aileen had called Mary a couple of times to complain about how much more she did in the house than Danny did, and Mary thought they'd be good friends after that, bonded by the exasperation their husbands caused them. But Aileen didn't want that kind of camaraderie. Now as she watched Aileen lean into Danny, she understood that her daughter's marriage was nothing like her own. Aileen had forgiveness in her and a determination for happiness that Mary didn't.

Mary watched as Aileen placed something in the casket. At the end of the night, Mary went up to say a last goodbye to Mike and saw that Aileen had left her love note on her father's chest.

On Thursday morning, Mary sat in the limousine and looked out the windows as they followed the hearse from the funeral parlor to the school. Aileen sat next to her with the baby in her lap; Danny held Tara's hand. Father Ahearn helped Mary out of the limousine, and quickly arranged a processional order. The baby squirmed, pulling at Aileen's dress, bunching it at her hip, and Mary reached over and tugged it down. She would have liked to carry the baby or have Tara's hand in hers, something warm and alive touching her.

At 10 a.m., with more light filtering into the school than had at the 7 a.m. Mass, the fluorescent lights on the shellacked yellow brick walls smacked Mary with the ungodliness of the place. This was not what Mike would have wanted. He would have wanted the dignity, the solemnity, the parade of an aisle in a church. Aileen was right. It wasn't the parish he loved so much, but the church itself, and for him the church was not in the people, as Father Ahearn had instructed at Mass the morning after the fire; it was in the altar, the pews, the aisle. She knew this now with a sickening certainty. Passing the office where the phone rang, and the custodian lounged, Mary, for Aileen's sake, pretended not to be bothered. A child, out of her classroom, cried at the sight of the coffin, and Mary realized, in horror, that school was in session.

They followed the coffin into the gym, and Mary watched as Aileen spotted the retracted basketball hoops. Between the rows of folding chairs, she found the black floor paint of foul lines. Mary was sure her daughter was also picking up the smells of perspiration, floor wax, and rubber intermingling with the incense. Aileen glanced to the right, locating the source of the rubber—a gated cage in the corner where twenty or twenty-five variously sized balls were stored—and when she turned back to her mother, her eyes, doleful and brimming, Mary could only look away.

Once seated, Mary tried to pray but again couldn't. A cold practicality, she realized, had allowed her to give her husband this preposterous funeral, as if it were nothing more than an item on a to-do list. That's what she had let her life become—a to-do list. And here is where that list of a life had gotten her and Mike. She reached out to pat the coffin but it was farther away than she estimated, and her hand swiped the air.

Mary tried to listen to Father Ahearn but an odor nagged at her attention, vague at first, then unmistakable. Fish cakes. The school children would be eating fish cakes for lunch.

After the Mass, Father Ahearn offered to show her the room where the church items that had been rescued were stored. "It'll take a few minutes for everyone to get their cars lined up to follow to the cemetery," he said. "You don't need to wait out there." He asked Aileen and Danny to come, too, but they declined saying the baby needed changing, and Mary was glad for a few minutes out of view of everyone who knew what kind of a funeral she had given her husband.

The smell of smoke was so strong in the small room that Mary put her hand up to cover her mouth and nose. The priest pointed out disfigured statues, a silver crucifix—the upper half of which had folded in the heat, sooty chalices, singed vestments. Mary viewed the objects with regret and shame. They seemed to chastise her, as if to say, "This is what it's come to." Father Ahearn picked up a small steel box for her to examine. "These are some remnants." He held up a length of splintering wood the size of his hand. "This is from one of the pews. There's glass from a window, and this is a tile from the floor. When we rebuild, we're going to bury the box at the foot of the new altar—a kind of symbolic foundation, the new church built on the old."

"That's lovely," Mary said.

He directed her attention to two gilded boxes. "We managed to save the relics, too—a bit of bone from St. Philip, a thread from the robe of St. Francis."

Mary came alive with an idea. She reached into her purse pretending she needed a tissue, opened her wallet, and pulled the caul into her palm. After pointing out the surviving Stations of the Cross, Father Ahearn advised, "We better go. The cars should be ready by now."

"Yes," Mary answered distractedly, moving back toward the steel box. She wanted to do something to make up for this funeral, to make up for the stingy to-do-list life she had given Mike. Something grand. When Father Ahearn turned to the door, she dropped the caul among the remnants.

Outside, a respectable number of cars had lined up to follow to the cemetery, and Mary was relieved. Worse than a funeral in a school gym would have been a burial no one attended. She settled herself into the limousine. Aileen was crying as she fed a bottle to Daniel Michael. Mary turned to her, about to announce what she had done, that one day Mike would be at the foot of the altar, a part of the new church's foundation. But Mary wasn't sure Aileen would approve. She'd wait, she decided, maybe until they rebuilt the church. Then she'd invite Aileen and her family to come for Mass—she'd have a Mass dedicated to Mike. And after Communion, after Aileen had stood at the foot of the altar, Mary would tell her. Or maybe she never would. Maybe it would be between her and Mike.

For now, she looked out the window, and cried for the loss of her husband.

PHLEBOTOMIST'S DAY

IT'S PHLEBOTOMISTS' DAY, KATE discovers when she enters the mall-like medical center. On a table near the elevator is balanced a folded piece of oak tag, and in the fashion of a sixth-grade language arts project, gold stars, curled ribbons, and artfully cut photographs of smiling women and a few men in white coats are glued on it. "Happy Phlebotomist's Day" is written in purple Magic Marker.

All the departments beckon with their doorlessness and uphol-stered mauve chairs: Radiology, Pharmacy, Ophthalmology. Things get more serious on the upper floors: Oncology on the fourth. But she's not going there. Not yet. Maybe never. It's just a lump. Probably a cyst. Just a cyst.

Her first stop, as instructed by her internist, Dr. Newman, is the lab. She has set up all her yearly appointments within a couple of weeks of each other. Gynecologist, mammogram, physical, derma-tologist, dentist. And the biopsy, just added to the schedule as a result of the mammogram. She thought of cancelling the physical and focusing all her mental energy on the upcoming biopsy, and now she can't remember why she didn't do that. She doesn't want to be here. She's told Rob and her daughter Jules nothing. No point in worrying them . . . if Rob would even worry—their marriage is that far gone.

"Hi. I'm Alina," a young woman says as she taps at a shadow of blue in the crux of Kate's arm.

"I have tricky veins," she warns the young woman. Survivalist veins. National Geographic veins. They lie still and visible until the predatory needle punctures the skin, then at the last moment, they roll out of the needle's path. It is an impressively protective reflex, which leaves the vial empty and the phlebotomist needing to stick her again.

"Don't worry," Alina says with all the confidence and goodwill of one being celebrated. "Make a fist." As the needle enters her arm, Kate looks over at the cheerful-looking, middle-aged woman in the cubicle next to her who is being attended to by a phlebotomist even younger than Kate's.

"Oops," Alina says. "You're right. Look at that."

Kate doesn't look; she continues to watch as the other woman's vials fill up. When the needle is removed, the woman shoots her arm straight up in the air. The gesture reminds Kate of something.

She glances at her empty tubing, looks away again at the arm in the air, prepares for the next stick. The woman is pointing to the ceiling, not at anything in particular, it's just the shape her fingers have taken. An image of Mr. Teller, Kate's elementary school choirmaster comes to mind. Dyed (the choir members suspected) black hair, belly over his belt, his arm in the air directing them to send their voices up to heaven.

"Got it."

Kate looks and sees her vial finally filling. "Good." And then a wave of vulnerability that masks as kindheartedness comes over her as it often does when she's having blood drawn. "Happy Phlebotomists' Day."

Alina tosses her head as though the whole thing is silly but Kate imagines her parents taking her out to a celebratory dinner later, though they might remind her that it's still not too late to become a doctor.

"You have a beautiful name," Kate adds. Another irrepressible urge—the loss of blood makes her want to say something that will make her seem kind. She thinks that if she had blood drawn every day, she'd be a better person.

When Kate stands to leave, the woman's arm is still in the air. She smiles but doesn't explain. Kate assumes it has something to do with her blood flowing too slowly, too quickly, too thinly, too thickly.

This isn't the only time Kate has thought of Mr. Teller. She has thought of him from time to time, most vividly years ago when she was at a performance of Handel's *Rinaldo*. She was dating Rob, beginning to think she would marry him, and because he had a much treasured subscription to City Opera passed down to him from his grandparents, she was doing her best to like opera. Music played a significant role in Rob's life and his family history—he and his parents and grandparents, as well as several aunts and uncles, had all taken piano or violin or voice lessons; one uncle played the accordion. They knew the names of composers and singers; they knew librettos and had heated arguments over whether Maria Callas or Renata Tebaldi was the better soprano. Kate knew David Bowie, The Band, The Rolling Stones. Rock and roll was integral to her life, but music had played no role in her family. No one played an instrument or took lessons. She remembered a ukulele, which of course, no one took seriously. There was a stereo console from Ethan Allen in the living room, and she could remember dusting it and the menagerie of glass animals her mother kept on it, but it wasn't until Rob once asked what kind of music her parents listened to that she realized she couldn't remember music ever coming from it. Rob committed himself to putting a variety of music in her life, and she committed to appreciating it, though after two operas—a four-hour version of *Le nozze de Figaro*, and an equally long *Don Giovanni*, she learned only that she hated Mozart. She was pretty sure she hated opera, too. Then he took her to see Handel's *Rinaldo*.

Dr. Newman asks about her sister.

Kate steadies herself. "She's back on chemo."

"I'm sorry."

She has bad veins, too. They've put a port in her chest to administer the chemo so they don't have to keep puncturing her. It's not supposed to hurt but it does, and she has nightmares of things crawling in and out of it.

"Are you having regular mammograms?"

"I have a lump," she blurts, though she hadn't planned on telling him. There's nothing he can do about it.

"Oh. Do you have a biopsy scheduled?"

"Yes."

Now he wants details—where, when. Does she want him to feel it?

No, she doesn't and she'd like to stop talking about it now. When he says, "Good luck," she thanks him, though she doesn't want to need luck.

At the end of Act One of *Rinaldo*, Almirena, Rinaldo's beloved, is abducted by a sorceress. Grief-stricken, Rinaldo beseeches her to return: *Cara sposa, amante cara, dove sei? Deh! Ritorna a' pianti miei! Del vostro Erebo sull'ara colla face del mio sdegno io vi sfido, o spirit rei.* My dear betrothed, my dear love, where are you? Come back at my tears. Evil spirits, I defy you with the fire of my wrath on your infernal altar.

As she listened for the first time, she remembered Mr. Teller. Rinaldo's was the type of voice Mr. Teller had, the voice he used in short bursts at choir practice, the voice he showcased at the school's annual talent show, the voice Kate and her classmates mocked mercilessly. They would form their mouths into wide O's, flutter their eyes and shriek silently in deprecating imitation. To them, he had the voice of a woman—high, sweet, feminine. Then someone would start with "Maybe he *is* a woman. A he/she." But Kate also remembered the parents at the talent show, the mothers and fathers who would close their eyes and let their heads gently sway as though they were floating on his voice. Even Kate's mother, who knew nothing about music, closed her eyes and was moved. And when Kate closed hers at the opera that night, Rinaldo's voice became what she had always imagined a soul to be, a soft mist rising toward the ceiling of the opera house, passing through the roof to the night sky, flying to heaven, sure of the way.

"Reach to heaven," Mr. Teller would encourage the choir at the high notes as he pointed, arm exaggeratedly upstretched. Kate could never hit the highest notes; she mouthed them, afraid that if she tried, the sound she emitted would get her excused from choir. That was how it worked; anyone could join but some would be excused. Usually, it was because of blatant misbehavior (she and her friends were discreet in their mockery) but sometimes it was because of the persistent flatness or tunelessness of a voice. Even though they all pretended to hate choir, it was a humiliation to be excused.

Kate was in her mid-twenties, years away from choir when Mr. Teller was murdered on his way home from the church one evening. It was vicious. A group of four teenage boys hit him, kicked him, all the while demanding that he say, "I'm a fucking faggot." When he finally did, one of the boys knifed him. They were caught—one confessed and gave the names of the others. The confessed had gone to Kate's school for a short time before being expelled. There were rumors that he had been excused from choir, but Kate couldn't imagine someone who could be a party to that act ever singing hymns.

At Mr. Teller's funeral—many of those who had mocked him, including Kate, went—an elderly nun spoke, remembering his pointing and saying that she liked to think that, at the moment of his death, he let his voice out, not in a scream but as a note on which to send his soul to heaven. It was his melodious soul that Kate thought of years later when she closed her eyes at *Rinaldo*.

Countertenor. That was the classification for Mr. Teller's and Rinaldo's voice. Rob bought her CDs of the opera that Christmas and asked her to be his *cara sposa* that spring.

The EKG is fine. Her weight, lungs, reflexes, ears are all fine. She can call the office in a few days for blood results.

"Good luck," Dr. Newman says again.

As she leaves the medical center, it occurs to her that Mr. Teller knew the limitations of her voice all along. But he also knew that at some point, she would need to send her voice and soul out, pleading toward heaven.

That evening at home, she puts on the CD of *Rinaldo*. She sings quietly, flatly, hoping her voice knows the way.

GRAVESTONES

"It's too far away," Jackie grieved as they drove. "I hate having him all the way out here alone."

"It's what he wanted," her husband Joe reminded her.

"It's all he could afford. All we could afford," she said of her father's government-paid-for plot in the military cemetery an hour from their home. He had stopped paying life insurance premiums and had, over the years, given everything he saved to Jackie's mother in a futile attempt to gain her back.

But when they arrived, parked, and started looking for his grave, a peacefulness came over her. "It's so egalitarian," she remarked, looking out on row after radiating row of stones, all of the same size, the same shape, spaced equally. Beautiful math. Equality making precise designs—perfectly straight rows if she looked this way, star shapes if she looked another. There was something eternal about it, too, something infinite. But most importantly, everyone was equal there. No greater or lesser people. She hadn't noticed that at his burial, and it was a surprise to her now given that it was a military cemetery and what was the military without rank, without men and women who didn't recognize their superiors? Not that her father would have minded having rank pulled. He had always been aware of being one of the "little guys," not a commanding officer, not the head supervisor at his job. He would have expected to have a small gravestone while the colonels and captains had more impressive ones. But on that first visit since his burial, Jackie had thought "thank God" because it would have broken her heart to have his importance diminished here, his life and service made into an equation that equaled a smaller stone. He hadn't minded being one of the "little guys" until the very end when the cancer had run rampant, suffocating the familiar cheer out of him, making him forget that he had always been satisfied, and turning him into someone who decided he hadn't amounted to much. But there he was, as good as anyone.

She carried a bouquet of carnations they had stopped for at a roadside stand, and a green plastic flower planter that she had discovered in a bin in the cemetery parking lot that she had mistaken for a garbage receptacle until she saw someone reach into it.

"Here he is," Joe pointed, finding the grave number on the back of the stone: 035697.

Jackie's tears were instantaneous. "I miss him."

"Me, too."

After a minute, she sniffed and wiped her eyes, bent down and poked the planter into the ground and worked the stems of the flowers into its narrow funnel. "It is peaceful, isn't it?" she asked, standing.

"It is," Joe assured her. "And this is where he belongs. He loved being in the Navy."

"I just feel lonely for him out here by himself." Her attention went to a little rock perched on his gravestone. She picked it up and examined it. "Look," she said, holding the rock between her thumb and forefinger. It was smooth and pearly, uneven in its shape.

Joe took the small stone and turned it over in his hand, examining it to discover why he was supposed to be impressed by it.

"It was right here." Jackie took it back and placed it on the right side of her father's gravestone.

"Hmm."

"I know the Jews do that," she said, "put little stones on the gravestone, don't they? I don't know what it means though."

"I think it just shows that someone visited," Joe suggested.

Jackie shook her head. "Nobody in my family has been out here. And he didn't have any friends at the end. He never kept in touch with people."

"I know," Joe agreed, "but someone visited him and put the stone there."

Jackie shook her head.

"Then how did it get there?"

"I don't know. A squirrel. Or the wind blew it."

Joe screwed up his face. "Why wouldn't you want to believe that someone came to visit him?"

"It's not that I don't want to believe it, it's just that I don't think that's what happened."

They looked at each other for a few moments then looked away.

"There's not much to do at a cemetery, is there?" Jackie said after a bit.

"Once when my mother, my uncle, and I visited my grandfather's grave, we had a picnic there."

"Really? Somehow I don't think this is that kind of cemetery."

She touched the engraved letters of her father's name. "Bye, Daddy."

They walked back to the car, reading the names off the gravestones. Albert Stines, Joseph Durango. Edward Lampel.

"It's not that I don't want people visiting him," she said, feeling a need to clarify her response. "I'd love it if I knew someone else was coming out here once in a while." She blinked her tears away.

Joe shrugged. "I'm just saying it's possible. Maybe someone read his obituary in the paper and came out here. He lived a long life. He met a lot of people."

Jackie took his hand and considered the idea of a visitor. A woman came to mind—someone vague, no one Jackie knew, just a creation of her imagination, someone to give to her father. To her surprise, she found that she liked that idea, and when they got into the car, she looked out the window as Joe drove, thinking more about this mysterious woman who was missing her father, visiting his grave, thinking enough of him to leave a little stone.

Once a week, Roberta Levine took the bus to the Pinelawn Cemetery. It wasn't that she had a husband there, though over the last few years of visiting, she had come to think of herself as a widow of sorts. There were even times when she almost believed it, one occasion when she actually told someone next to her on the bus that she was a widow just to try out the feel of the words. But she still knew the truth. "I'm not senile," she'd sometimes say to herself. "Not yet." The truth was that she had never married. It just happened that way, as it does sometimes with women, men, too. And overall, she didn't mind. Work; that had been the key. As long as she kept busy, she could pretend she didn't notice the loneliness.

And now, in a way, the worst of being unmarried was over. It was so much harder to be young and alone than old and alone. She didn't have to explain anymore why she never married; people didn't ask. But how many times had she been asked in the past? As if she knew the answer. "Oh, the right man never came along." Or "Oh, I haven't given up yet." Or "I guess I just haven't gotten around to it." Most of the women she knew now were alone, too— widowed or divorced. Some of them had even been widowed longer than they had been married. And they had all gotten used to being alone, as she had. But few of them kept as busy as she did.

When she retired from the insurance company, she started volunteering. First, it was at a public school. She had believed that worse than not marrying was not having children. But, though she stayed with it for two years, she learned quickly that she didn't get along with children with all their smartmouths and answering back and not knowing that adults were to be respected. After that, she read to patients in the hospital for a while until her mother became infirm, and then she spent the next year caring for her. After her mother died, Roberta volunteered in a nursing home, but after a few miserable months, she realized she wanted nothing more to do with old, helpless people. What patience she had for them was used up on her mother.

Having run through the spectrum of ages of people, Roberta was stumped as to where she'd volunteer next. She never liked animals, so any kind of work with dogs or cats was out. She bounced from place to place for a while, trying to find the right fit: she helped out when the synagogue ran special events; she worked for a few hours a day in her local library. But none of it really satisfied her, and in fact, the effort wore her down. She didn't like people anymore, she was beginning to realize, sadly. But maybe that was natural for a woman who had spent so much time on her own.

She stopped volunteering but the days at home were long, even though she broke them up with a walk in the morning and one in the afternoon. It was on one of these walks that she had a realization. It wasn't that she didn't like people, per se; it was just that she didn't have the resources for all the needing that people did. That's when it occurred to her that Pinelawn Cemetery was only a short bus ride away. They could probably use volunteers to tend the graves, to put poppies out on Memorial Day and Veterans Day. There she could satisfy her need to keep useful, and the people wouldn't demand anything from her.

Roberta was assigned sections M, N, O, and P. The coordinator had been concerned that this might be too large an area for her; they both looked at the sections on the map of the cemetery, but Roberta decided that with all the walking she had been doing lately, she was in shape for it. She was to pick up any flower arrangements left at graves, and return the green plastic planters to the bins in each section. There were to be no wilting or dead flowers, as this would detract from the dignity of the place.

Roberta walked her rows deliberately, forcing herself not to rush ahead when she spotted a bouquet, careful not to overlook anything that would compromise the cemetery's austere beauty—a tissue, a mint wrapper that blew out of someone's hand. She found the work so satisfying and calming, not at all depressing as she fleetingly wondered if it might be.

After a few weeks, she started to become familiar with the names on the graves, able to recite some of them as she approached. She made it a kind of exercise, memorizing a few names a week, knowing that it was important for someone her age to keep her mind active.

James Riley arrived at the cemetery sometime in the winter or early spring of the second year that Roberta had been volunteering. After a bout with pneumonia that fall, she couldn't risk going out of the house more than was necessary, so stayed away from the cemetery until the weather warmed up and some of her strength returned.

She recognized the name on the gravestone immediately and the date of his birth made him the right age. From time to time she still thought about him. He had asked her to dance and she said no. Not that she didn't want to—she very much did—but she thought he had been too forward, putting his arm around her waist as if they were already a couple. "Not just yet," she remembered saying, smiling as she lifted his hand from her hip. James Reilly. He was everything she wanted—tall and handsome with his black hair and blue eyes, charming and funny. More than anything she wanted a man who could make her laugh and sensed he could do that. She was twenty; he was older. The marrying among her friends had begun and she still believed her time would come, too, and soon. She was full of expectation and confidence with her full figure, thick brown hair and large dark eyes. And she had had those eyes on James Reilly for a while. And then she finally caught his attention. She had been stopping in at the pharmacy where he worked for one item or another on a regular basis, and he'd finally asked her name. When she noticed the poster in his window announcing a Knights of Columbus dance, she asked, as casually as she could, if he'd be going. "I will be, and you should come," he said and winked. So, though it wasn't a place where her mother wanted her to go looking for a boy—"you won't find a Jewish boy there; they're all Catholics"—she had gone.

"Not just yet," she had said, and he smiled too, as she took his hand from her waist. She expected him to come back; she might have even said confidently to a friend, "He'll be back." But he didn't come back. He found someone else to dance with, and someone else after that—a petite blonde. Roberta kept an eye on him all night. He asked the same blonde to dance three dances in a row then steered her to the refreshment table with his hand at her mid-back. If any of the men who asked Roberta to dance that night were interested in her, she didn't notice because she couldn't take her attention off Jimmy. At one point, she caught his eye, and he nodded a happy hello to her and gave her a thumbs-up, which she wasn't sure how she was supposed to read: approval of her dance partner, approval of his dance partner, an acknowledgment that he knew he was supposed to come back and ask her again, a sign that he would be back. But he didn't come back; she waited through the last dance, and even though she didn't want to see it, she couldn't help herself from watching him hold his blonde friend's coat as she slipped gracefully into it, watching them link themselves together as he offered his arm and she took it.

Roberta didn't stop going to the pharmacy—she didn't want to appear the sore loser. Actually, at first she kept going, hoping that if she kept herself in his sight he'd turn to her when his romance soured. Instead, when he saw her next, he thanked her. "I never thought being turned down for a dance would be the best thing that ever happened to me," he said, with a laugh. "If you hadn't turned me down, I might not have met Janet. Isn't it funny how things happen?" He went on to suggest that she hadn't done so badly herself, apparently referring to one of the men he saw her dance with. She smiled and played along, "Not too badly."

Of course, he and Janet married.

Roberta told herself it wouldn't have worked between them anyway, he being Catholic and she, Jewish. But that was only her trying to make herself feel better. It would have worked wonderfully.

Isn't it funny? She thought about that for a long time afterwards. Isn't it funny how a chance comes once? Isn't it funny how a person could not know that? How with one silly move, one silly answer, a person's future could be determined? She could have said yes to him when he asked. Everything would have been different. They would have danced all night. Someone else would have asked his blonde to dance; someone else would have asked his blonde to marry him. But that's not what happened; what happened was that she said, "not just yet," so coyly, so confidently.

She might not have suffered so much except that after him, there weren't many others, none that she really cared for, anyway. It was as if she threw away, not just a chance at him, but all her chances. How was she to know that "not just yet" would be her one great regret?

Even though there were probably thousands of James Reillys in the world, maybe even a hundred right there in the cemetery, certainly more than one, more than a few, she decided this was him. Still, she thought she might make that a project—walk through the entire cemetery a couple of sections at a time and count up the James Reillys. Jimmy Reillys. But no, she didn't want to do that. She wanted only this James Reilly who had come to her section. O35697.

She stopped by to see him every time she visited the cemetery. Sometimes she pretended they had been married, that the night she turned him down was a joke between them, that he had pursued her despite her protests and had won her. Sometimes she pretended some of the men in other plots were jealous. Albert Stines, Joseph Durango—she liked that name—would complain that she paid Jimmy more attention than she paid them. They had reason to be jealous, she would have admitted. She never anticipated seeing them the way she anticipated seeing him. Jimmy could still make her pulse jump, even in his grave; Albert and Joseph never did.

Roberta's pneumonia returned that fall after she tramped around the cemetery after a hard rain and sat on the crowded bus with wet feet. She disliked being so undependable, letting the volunteer coordinator down like that again. It was best, she decided, if she resigned, since she couldn't tell when she'd be up and around again.

Eventually she recovered, but she never regained her full strength, and in fact, she believed her body was beginning to fail. Staunchly, she contacted the graduated care facility she had inquired about a few years earlier. She did not want to die alone; she did not want to fall and break her hip and be on the floor for days, or have a heart attack or a stroke and be helpless in her apartment. She wished it were otherwise; she wished she could stay home and be cared for by someone who loved her, but she wasn't one of those people that would happen for. And she did want to be cared for even if she had to pay for it. The grounds at the facility were grassy; there was even a little pond. The staff provided plenty of activities—trips to Atlantic City, and regular buses into town for shopping and temple. Maybe she'd volunteer to organize games or tend the garden.

Before she moved in, she took a trip to the cemetery. As she walked toward Jimmy, she felt the restfulness of the place embrace her. She wished she could be buried there. But that wasn't to be. Only the servicemen and servicewomen and their spouses had that right. She would go into the plot that her father bought so long ago—a family plot—like a little girl crawling into her parents' bed.

And Jimmy's wife? That blonde? What had become of her? Roberta wondered. She wasn't buried with him. Not yet. But she did have the right to be. She'd lie with him there eventually, a part of the quiet grandeur of the place.

It didn't matter now. Roberta wasn't jealous of her anymore. It only mattered that the thought of Jimmy filled her with company, and she could remember it anyway she wanted to. What difference did it make now? She remembered dancing with him. She had seen it in her mind so many times. Yes, she remembered the swirl of the room, the perspiration off his sideburns, the sweet smokiness of his breath, his hand at her back.

She stood at his grave, remembering, smiling. She'd miss him. But she was glad to have had her time with him. She bent down and picked up a little rock from the ground—a little gift for him. A goodbye gift.

"I'd love to dance, Jimmy," she whispered as she placed the rock on his gravestone.

A MATTER OF FAITH

THE FIRST TIME THE Virgin Mary appeared to me, I told her to go away. I was in bed alone. Tim was out on the couch. Though he didn't know it yet, I had been toying with the idea of ending our marriage—two years of sleeping in separate rooms. I had been in bed nearly two hours, the usual time it took me to fall asleep, when I heard my name.

"Regina."

It came from within me and from without, from the deep place in my chest where a bronchial cough would reverberate—and indeed my chest did seem to resonate—and at the same time, from the side of the room where a small TV sat on a low dresser, the side I was not facing. Somehow, I knew not to open my eyes. I imagined that that was the same counterintuitive instinct that once kept me from slamming on the brakes when my car went into a skid. Yet, I was aware of a light, not filling the room—this wasn't a grand entrance—but insinuating a soft glow just over my shoulder.

I don't know how I knew it was her, but the same way my name emanated from my chest, her identity emanated from that soft glow, and I knew I just wasn't up to seeing her. Once you've seen the Virgin Mary, you're expected to do something impressive on her behalf, build a church, for example. I had been to Lourdes where she appeared to Bernadette. "Drink the water, eat the grass, build a church," she is said to have demanded. So they built one, and everyone who goes there fills up little virgin-shaped bottles of the healing water. I did it, too; I had a sick sister at home. I don't know what she meant about the grass; it must have been some misunderstanding on Bernadette's part. But I certainly wasn't up to building a church; I wasn't even up to going to one. And I wasn't up to having the Virgin Mary try to talk me out of my thoughts of divorce, not yet when I had just begun entertaining them, and that's the other thing I thought she might have in mind—to make me the little wave on which the tide of broken marriages might end; I didn't want to get all wrapped up in the awe of seeing her and end up promising something I'd regret. So I asked her to go away. A few years previous, after I'd had a dream that my friend gave birth to a baby girl and it turned out to be true, I read a book on developing my psychic abilities. The author warned that in trying to open up psychic pathways, one might be visited by guides from other planes. If I wasn't ready to receive the guide, I was to tell it kindly to go away. That is what I told the Virgin Mary. I made my request sound like something from the Mass: I'm not ready to receive you now. According to the book, if the spirit guide who visited was a manifestation of positive energy, it would honor my request to leave. Mary went away.

In the morning, there was no physical sign of her—no flower, or scent, or residual light. But I did wake with my mind clearly made up on the divorce.

The next time she came to me, I was six years away from Tim and four years into my second marriage. Derek and I never slept in separate rooms, and falling asleep was only taking me thirty to forty minutes instead of the two hours it took when I was with Tim. Mary came the same way she had come before, calling me from inside and out, and I recognized her immediately.

"Regina."

Derek didn't hear her, probably because he's Protestant, not Catholic like me.

At first, I didn't respond—didn't ask her to go, didn't open my eyes to acknowledge her. Over the years, I had only thought vaguely about what I'd do if she came again. In a way, I'd come to disbelieve her visitation, view it as a hypnagogic dream, or an intuitive moment when I appeared outside myself to guide myself to a difficult decision. But now that she was here again, I knew this wasn't a dream, nor was it some higher version of myself that I was seeing, and I knew, too, that it'd be spiritually risky to be so dismissive of her again.

I opened my eyes. And squinted. Mary was not as vibrant as I expected her to be. In fact, her image was so fuzzy that I fumbled for my glasses, which I realized, after dropping a box of tissues and my bottle of melatonin, I had left on the bathroom sink. My first response to her, then, was slight annoyance. Why couldn't she punch up the vision of herself a little so an astigmatic like myself could get a clear look? What I could make out was the light around her head. Like the last time, it was not a fiery light, but a modest glow. She seemed older than me, and I liked that, as Derek was younger which hadn't mattered until a month before when I turned forty, and he still had three years of his thirties to go. She had on a gown, I think, something long and white. She hovered near the closet, on Derek's side, the sliding door of which wasn't completely closed, and I could see the outline of his shirts behind her. On my side of the closet, also not completely closed, a bra dangled from the door handle.

I was prepared for her to ask something of me. This was a Bronx apartment. She could have asked me to drink the water like she asked of Bernadette in Lourdes—Bronx water is quite drinkable. But if she had made any demands about grass, I couldn't have obliged. It wasn't that there wasn't any. There are parks and patches of green here and there, but who in their right mind would pick something up from the ground in the Bronx and eat it, even for the Virgin Mary? And as far as building a church went, I made up my mind that I'd reason with her. There wasn't an inch of space to build on anywhere in the neighborhood, and even if there were, there was already enough noise without adding construction to it. Besides, there were plenty of churches, including an Immaculate Conception only a few blocks away.

I lay there gazing in an unfocused way at her, prepared to hear her demands. But she asked nothing of me and eventually, I yielded to a restless sleep.

"The Virgin Mary came to me last night," I told Derek in the morning.

"Didn't she come to you once before?" He was already up, showered, standing at the closet choosing a shirt.

"You remember me telling you that?"

"I remember everything you tell me."

"She came just before I started my divorce. But I told her to go away."

"What did you tell her this time?" He pulled out a grey shirt.

"I didn't tell her anything. I just looked at her and then fell asleep."

"Hmm. Do I need to iron this?"

"I can't see. Bring it here." I looked over the shirt. "Not if you're wearing a jacket."

"Good."

"She was right there by your side of the closet."

"Really?" He didn't seem particularly impressed. He put on his shirt and returned to the bathroom.

Momentarily, I was offended by his cavalier attitude toward the Virgin's appearance, but unlike in my first marriage where Tim and I assumed the worst about each other's intentions first, fought over it, and apologized later, with Derek, I had learned not to be so quickly injured. Virgin Mary or not, Derek worked at home two days a week, but on the other three, he had to be in the office at 8:30 a.m. and his mind was on his forty-five-minute commute. I couldn't blame him.

She came to me again a couple of days later. It was late, and I was just beginning to stop anticipating her. I'd turned my back to the place where she had appeared and had closed my eyes when the glow announced her arrival. I turned toward her, and I think she looked right at me, but again, she asked nothing.

In the morning, I called to Derek over the noise of the shower. "I saw her again. I think she's going to keep coming."

"What?" he stuck out his head, and I kissed his wet face.

"She came again last night. Mary."

He ducked back into the spray. "What do you want to do about it?" he gurgled. Derek was an activist in the sense that he believed one should show resistance even if the forces one was resisting were virtually unmovable. When the sirens got too frequent and too loud in our neighborhood, he called the assemblyman, the councilman, the fire and police departments. When delivery trucks arrived at 5 a.m. at the nursing home next door, he called the supervisor of the home and the owners of the trucking company. And when car alarms went off incessantly on the street, he pitched eggs out the window at the offending vehicles.

"I don't know." I put the lid down and sat on the toilet.

"Shouldn't you tell someone?"

"I don't want to get a bunch of priests involved."

"Do you think this counts as a miracle?"

"I guess so. I don't really know what constitutes a miracle."

"Don't people flock to the places where she's been?" he asked.

"Yes, and I don't want people flocking here. Do you?"

"Well, we'd have to turn that side of the room into a shrine. We could empty the closet and make a little grotto, like at Lourdes."

He stepped out of the shower, and I handed him a towel. "What do you know about Lourdes?"

"I'm a Protestant. I'm not ignorant. I know about Lourdes."

"I was at Lourdes, you know."

"You told me. There were people there who were lighting huge candles."

"The size of Duraflame logs. And one woman dragged a photo across the walls of the grotto. I was behind her, and I was so curious that I didn't pay any attention to the grotto at all. I just wanted to get a look at that photo. I finally got a glimpse; it was of a bride. I was supposed to be praying for my intentions. My sister had the cancer then. But I couldn't pray. I just kept wondering what was wrong with that bride. Anyway, why doesn't Mary go back there?"

"Because she must want to appear to you."

"Why?"

"I don't know. Maybe you're supposed to be some kind of a messenger."

"I don't want to be a messenger."

"You may not have a choice."

Later that morning, another unusual thing happened. My neighbor from down the hall, a guy I called the Pentacostalist, exited his apartment, locked his door, and walked slowly toward the elevator where I was waiting. What was strange was that he usually ducked into the stairway or back into his apartment at the sight of me. I think it had something to do with Derek and I living together before we were married. He had judged me as a sinner. Either that or he found me attractive and judged himself as a sinner. As always, he had his Bible with him. Though as far as I could tell he was utterly devoid of charisma, he had some idea that he was a preacher. On Sundays, through our open windows, Derek and I could hear the singing of hymns coming from his apartment. Apparently, he invited friends or family to his "church" to worship with him. Derek suspected there was something illegal about the use of the apartment for that, and he intended to get around to investigating it. He also objected to the "Say Yes to Jesus" bumper sticker that the Pentacostalist had carefully centered above his peephole, as it was against building regulations to attach anything permanent to the doors.

Unfortunately for the Pentacostalist, our schedules coincided quite often. I'd leave the apartment in the morning, and hear the locks opening on his door. He'd come out, see me, go back in. But it was when we met in the lobby that I took a smug pleasure in his holier-than-thou commitment. He'd look at me, look at his Bible, measure the strength of his will against the flaccidity of his quadriceps—we lived on the eighth floor, and refusing to get into an elevator with me meant walking up all those stairs. But he held firm, though sometimes I think he ducked into the stairwell, came out when I was gone, and rang for the next elevator.

This morning, he didn't go back inside, didn't duck into the stairwell. Instead, he moved slowly toward me, watching the greasy-looking waxed tile floor, then placing himself a good distance away. I wondered if this was some kind of test he was putting himself through. Once in the elevator, he studied the cover of his Bible until the opening door released him into the lobby.

After the Virgin's first visit I told only a couple of people I had seen her. "You?" my friend, who had gone back to school to study theology, asked in offended amazement. "I'm dedicating all my energy to the study of Catholicism, and the Virgin appears to you?" And when I told this friend that because I had woken up afterwards so sure that I should divorce Tim that maybe Mary had come to help guide me to that decision, she was relieved. "Well, if that's what you think, then you didn't see the Virgin Mary. Mary is against divorce."

My mother, who had, since her retirement, kept busy in her local church, was also puzzled. "Why do you think she came to you, dear?" she asked. I told her I didn't know, that if things happened fairly, Mary would have appeared to her, and my mother humbly agreed. I don't think she believed I had a real visitation, but after that, she became something of a Virgin Mary buff, tracking Her appearances, keeping me informed of them, and organizing trips to some of the more local sightings. At one point, she talked seriously about going to Medjugorje though each time she mentioned it, she pronounced Medjugorje differently. But conveniently, a woman on a farm in Ohio began having visitations, and my mother opted for the domestic trip. When she returned home with bags of corn for the priests in her church and for me, she told me about a hair that had fallen from the Virgin's head and how it had been preserved in a vial for all the pilgrims to view. "But it was so blonde, I could barely see it," my mother admitted, disappointedly.

"The Virgin wasn't a blonde," I pointed out.

"I didn't think so either," she mused.

I hadn't told my mother about Mary's return visits to me fearing that the unfairness of it would turn her against Mary or me altogether. But I was beginning to feel that I should tell someone other than Derek, that not telling was somehow blasphemous. I was supposed to testify, I knew that. That was the only reason Mary came to people: so they would attest to it.

That evening when I returned home, the Pentacostalist was in the hallway upstairs again. He acted as though he had been waiting for the elevator, and stepped toward it as the door opened, but I had the sense he had been lingering outside my apartment.

All at once, I suspected that he knew about Mary, and as I unlocked my door, I began to feel accused by him for keeping it a secret. Without any warning that I was about to do this, I blurted, "I saw the Virgin Mary." Then I stepped inside and slammed the door.

It was both a relief to have told someone and a burden. I couldn't have explained to Derek why I chose the Pentacostalist when we both considered him a freak. The only thing I could figure was that for some reason, Mary wanted the Pentacostalist to know, and she had moved through me and used me as a vehicle to shout out the news to him.

I tried to stay off the topic with Derek that night. "So, is the job going to continue to let you do two days a week at home?" I asked of his relatively new work arrangement.

"It looks that way." We were in the kitchen; Derek was making rice and beans. "They may even want to increase my time at home to three days. I think they think they get more hours out of me that way."

"Do you have work to do tonight?"

"A little. But listen, I was thinking about this Virgin Mary thing. Didn't you say that the first time she came to you, it was to guide you through your divorce?"

"I said that, but I don't know if that's why she really came. And I don't want to talk about it tonight."

"All right." But he persisted. "Just let me follow this through. Let's say that is why she came, to guide you. So why is she here now?" He raised his eyebrows. "You're not thinking of divorcing me, are you?"

"Yeah, right."

He looked at me as though he almost believed it was possible.

"I love you," I reminded him. "You know that." I kissed him, and he smiled and poured a little vinegar over the beans.

"She didn't come last night," I told the Pentacostalist when I saw him outside my door in the morning.

He looked down on the ground and stammered. "Can . . . may I see her?"

"What?" He was an unfortunately unattractive man—pocked skin, fat fingers.

"May I see her?"

"I said she didn't come." I pressed for the elevator and regretted confiding in him. There was no way he had known she had come to me, I realized, listening to him breathing through his mouth.

"May I see the spot where she appeared?"

I thought of the bedroom—bed unmade, smelling like sleep, dresser drawers half-closed. And the rest of the apartment—cereal bowls in the sink, wet towels thrown over the shower rod. "No."

"I'll pay you," he mumbled.

I pressed for the elevator again. "Pay me?"

"And I can get other people from my church to pay, too."

"Your church?" I sneered.

"'Wherever two or three are gathered in My name . . .'"

"Don't quote the Bible to me. I don't want your friends lining up here in front of my apartment. Okay? I mean it. I don't want anyone to know about this. I shouldn't have even told you."

"You haven't told anyone else?" he asked, lifting his eyes so that for the first time, he looked directly at me.

I pressed for the elevator again. "This thing is so damn slow," I mumbled. "No, I haven't told anyone else. Just my husband. And I don't want anyone else to know."

"You must share Her with the people," he demanded. "You must . . ."

The elevator finally arrived. "I have to go to work," I said, "and I don't want you standing outside my apartment all day."

As the door began to close, and I looked out at his determined face, I could picture his congregation gathered outside my door, the other neighbors coming into the hallway to see what all the commotion was about. I could see the super being called up, maybe the police, and I stuck my foot out just before the elevator door closed. "All right, let me straighten up a little," I said. "But if I show you, you can't tell anyone. That's the deal. If you do tell, I'll just deny it. I'll say you've been harassing me. Understand?"

"I just want to see."

I left the apartment door ajar, went in and quickly made the bed, threw the windows open to air the room out, hung the towels back on the rack, ran water into the cereal bowls. "Okay," I said when I went back to the door. "But there's nothing to see."

He squeezed his Bible in both hands. "That's fine. I just want to stand in the place where She was."

I led him into the room and pointed toward the closet; Derek's sneaker stuck out on his side.

"Here?" he asked.

"Right there."

He stood in the spot. "Here?"

"Yeah." He adjusted his position, secured his stance, then closed his eyes and held his Bible up. I waited for what I thought was a polite amount of time, nearly a minute, and then said, "Hey." I didn't know his name. I imagined Derek coming back having forgotten a file and seeing this guy and me exiting our bedroom. What would he think? Not that we had slept together; it was too preposterous. Still, the image of your wife coming out of your bedroom with another man was one a husband should be spared from seeing. "Hey. Time to go." He continued to stand there, calling on the Virgin, I suppose, trying to feel her presence. I poked him. "Hey." He came out of his trance.

He stepped off the spot as though he were stepping out of mud, lifting one foot, then planting it, lifting the other.

"Did you feel anything?" I asked.

He hesitated, then answered. "I don't know. Have you cleaned this area?"

"What do you mean?"

"Have you cleaned there?"

"I vacuum my house once a week," I said, though it was often more like once every two weeks.

"I don't know. I just don't think you should clean this spot. You might wash away some evidence."

"Why would I need evidence?"

He shrugged.

I was reminded of one of my mother's pilgrimages. "You know a woman in Ohio says she has a hair that fell out of Mary's head when She visited her."

"I heard about the Ohio visitations."

"You did?"

"May I look?" he glanced at the floor.

"You can look, but you'd probably only find my hair. They say that it's normal to lose as many as two hundred a day." I knew that because I had asked the woman who cuts my hair when I started finding hair on the bathroom floor. I looked at the Pentacostalist's balding head and realized how many hairs two hundred must sound like to him. "I have very thick hair," I added.

He got on his knees in a bowing position—head down, butt up--and examined the floor.

"But that woman in Ohio found a blonde hair," I continued. "I couldn't make out Mary's hair when she came to me, but I think that it's brown, isn't it?"

"Get a tissue," he ordered, pressing his fingers on a spot on the floor and turning them over to scrutinize something that had stuck to them.

I complied, though with a couple of sheets of toilet paper as we were out of tissues.

He placed something on the paper, handed it to me, then awkwardly pushed himself up off the floor.

I was looking down at a single strand of blonde hair against the backdrop of two sheets of toilet paper.

"Do you think it's Mary's?" the Pentacostalist asked.

I couldn't answer.

"Here," he said. "Wait here. I have something at home."

I stood frozen, staring at the blonde strand, natural blonde, I registered, noting the root.

The Pentacostalist brought back a small glass tube full of red strands of saffron. "I'll throw these out." He went into the bathroom and in a minute, brought back an empty, rinsed vial. "Put it in here."

I fed the strand into the vial.

"Now you have a relic, too."

I looked at him and couldn't tell if he was being sarcastic or not, if he was wondering what I was wondering: was this the Virgin Mary's hair or the hair of some woman Derek had slept with right here in our bedroom? Had it fallen out of Mary's head while she hovered at the closet glowing toward me, or had it fallen out of some woman's head while she was standing naked, early one afternoon, examining Derek's shirts while he was supposed to be working at home? I had a feeling I had seen the last of Mary. She wouldn't be back to answer my questions. It was a matter of faith now.

SEAMUS

Deidre always wanted a redheaded baby, but when Seamus was born, his hair obviously orange even though it was darkened and plastered to his head with placental fluid, Deidre's first response was panic.

Her eyes darted to Phillip, her brown-haired husband. His eyes moved from the baby to her. She was guilty and caught. The baby's hair was not hers and not Phillip's. Though Irish, she was not aware of any redheads in her family. Phillip's Italian family had none, either. It was her first love Sean's lush, auburn hair.

Then she did the math, or more precisely, her sense of time began to function properly. Sean had been dead eight years. Deidre and he had split up a year before that. She recovered and smiled at Phillip.

A nurse said, "Look at that hair. Where did that come from?" The other nurse leveled her gaze at her, as if to remind the inquisitive nurse that this was something they all had been instructed in, that it was in the handbook of delivery decorum: *Do not mention anything about which parent the baby looks like or doesn't look like. Be especially discreet if the baby looks like neither parent or appears to be of a race other than the parents'.*

Phillip said, "Well, you always loved red hair. You must have wished it into your DNA."

Deidre wondered if it were possible.

"Seamus?" Deidre asked, hopefully.

It was not Phillip's favorite name, but it had been Deidre's since she was eighteen years old and heard Sean refer to an Uncle Seamus in Ireland. "With that red hair, of course." Phillip bent and kissed her on the forehead.

When Phillip left, Deidre held Seamus and blew gently across his head, lifting the fine red hairs, whispering a "hi" to both her son and to Sean, whom she believed was somewhere smiling at her and this child.

At home, Seamus was active—kicking, wriggling—always wanting to move his body as though he were making up for his confinement in the womb, though he had been active in there, too. Deidre pumped his legs, jumped him up and down on the couch, gave him gentle pushes to help him roll over. As soon as he could hold his head up, she put him in his walker and in his bouncy swing. She jogged with him in the stroller; he laughed when she sprinted, loving the speed. She sensed a natural athleticism in him, the kind of athleticism Sean had had.

In the evenings, when Phillip arrived home from work, he did the fatherly tossing of Seamus in the air and flying him in circles. Seamus loved it, and one night, Phillip remarked to Deidre that she was good about letting him roughhouse with him, that he had expected her to be more cautious.

"I did, too," she answered. "But I don't want to stifle him. I think he's going to be athletic."

"Like us," Phillip said, proud of their genetics.

They were fit; they jogged and worked out but neither of them played a sport; neither had been high school or college athletes. Sean, who had played college and semi-pro hockey, semi-pro softball, and golf had had the kind of athleticism Deidre saw in Seamus.

When they put him to bed together later, Phillip smiled down at Seamus and said with amusement, "He really doesn't look like us, does he?"

She found herself thinking about Sean more than she had in years. And one morning, out of exhaustion, or some postpartum mind alteration, or just because the red hair constantly reminded her, she dropped into a fantasy in which Seamus was Sean's child. In this daydream, she wasn't married to Sean; he was still dead. She wasn't married to Phillip, either. She was raising Seamus alone; there was a romanticism in that she liked.

After that first time, the reveries would come quietly and often—little journeys that added dimension to her days. She enjoyed these daydreams and told herself it was only natural that Seamus's red hair would trigger such memories and fantasies. But then, other times, her enjoyment would be spoiled by guilt: these weren't things she should be thinking. On those occasions, she might call Phillip at work to bring herself back to her actual family. But the daydreams kept returning.

When at six months old, Seamus crawled backwards before learning to crawl forwards, Deidre felt a moment of panic. As a defenseman on his hockey teams, Sean had skated backwards with the coordination and speed of someone who was born to move in the world that way. She sat on the floor of the living room that first day of Seamus' backward locomotion knowing that somehow Sean was part of this child and wondering how it was possible. "Where are you?" she asked aloud.

She had been magnetized by Sean the first time she saw his auburn hair while he worked at the deli in her Bronx neighborhood. She found herself on tiptoes leaning into the high counter as she ordered a sandwich, feeling a pull from him and an immediate need to make physical contact. He leaned toward her, too. They were seventeen and neither of them had any sexual experience, but they learned with each other, spending hours in rented motel rooms, or in their bedrooms when their parents were out, tracing the mountains and valleys of each other's body, the taut and the soft. When he entered her, it was as if he took her home, a primal home she hadn't known she had been separated from until he brought her back there. If anyone had told her that after a time, it was natural in relationships for physical desire to wane, she wouldn't have been able to imagine it.

When she got pregnant. Sean said it was her decision, her body; he'd go along with whichever decision she made. She chose abortion, thinking that was what was best for them, that that was what he wanted. He admitted that he was relieved. (Sometimes in her reveries in which Seamus was Sean's baby, she imagined Seamus as this child, born instead of aborted. Other times, she imagined that child at the age he would be now and as Seamus's older brother.)

A year later, they broke up. A year after that, he was dead. A freak accident—slipped on the ice, not on a rink, but on a patch of black ice in the street while he was crossing, fell, hit his head hard on the curb. Drunk.

She began to think about reincarnation. Was it possible that Sean had been reincarnated in Seamus? There were nights when she desperately wanted to tell Philip what was on her mind. She thought it was almost possible for him to understand. He knew how deeply she had loved Sean, though he preferred to dismiss it as puppy love. But each night, she didn't dare.

She had started supplementing her breastfeeding with formula shortly after Seamus was born; he was a hungry baby. Having Seamus at her breast sometimes gave her a physical pleasure that made her squeamish. She googled it and learned that it wasn't unusual. But once the idea was in her head that Sean was somehow linked to Seamus, she couldn't stop connecting that pleasure to the memory of the pleasure Sean could arouse in her with just a flick of his tongue to the tip of her nipple. When she heard herself emit a quiet moan when Seamus latched on one evening, she panicked and pulled him off her. After that, she stopped breastfeeding and switched Seamus to formula and baby food, telling Phillip that Seamus needed the denser calories.

One night while they were watching TV in bed, she asked, "How do you think it happens? Seamus. His soul. His personality. All of it." She had to share something of her wonderings with him.

"Where is this coming from?" he asked, amused.

"I don't know. I guess it's the whole idea of birth. . . it's so amazing."

"It's a miracle."

"I know but . . ."

He turned to her and smiled impishly. "I know how it happened." He wriggled a hand between her thighs.

"I'm tired." But her body responded. She moaned when he sucked on her neck. Their lovemaking was tender and quiet— satisfying but not the lovemaking she'd had with Sean.

She wavered between believing it was possible that Seamus had some of Sean in him and believing she was going out of her mind. Finally, on a Saturday when she was feeling especially uncertain and vulnerable, while Phillip was out for a jog with Seamus, she called Vicky, a mutual friend of hers and Sean's who had kept her informed of his drinking binges after the breakup, the friend who called to say he was dead. Deidre carefully felt her out.

"Sometimes, I think I see Sean in the baby," she admitted.

"I'm not surprised," Vicky responded matter-of-factly. "You never got over him. So, maybe you're projecting him onto your son."

"What do you mean—projecting?"

"I don't think you ever resolved things. I don't think you ever made peace with leaving him. You felt guilty about that. You felt guilty about his death. And the baby . . . the baby you guys aborted. Your baby is bound to remind you of that. Especially since he has red hair."

Deidre could feel the tears coming. She acknowledged to herself that she had pushed forward away from the abortion, then away from the breakup, and away from Sean's death. All that pushing away had ended up pushing her back to Sean. But there was no more Sean.

"This was bound to catch up to you," Vicky pressed on. "I mean . . . you know Seamus is not Sean's baby. So, what else could it be?" And then in a lighter tone she added, "Unless sperm lives for years inside a woman's body. Maybe some of Sean's sperm hid somewhere inside you. That'd be just like him, wouldn't it? If anyone could pull something like that off, Sean could. He was always pulling some surprise on you."

She had almost forgotten that about Sean but now it came back to her. There were tickets to The Rolling Stones and dozens of other concerts, little presents inside big boxes, mystery vacations with her begging like a child to be told where they were going.

"He loved you so much."

"I know."

"Maybe you just need to mourn."

When Deidre hung up, Vicki texted, "You can always do a DNA test to see if Sean managed to pull this off. Lol."

Deidre googled DNA testing. She could send away for a kit; that was easy enough but she couldn't get a sample of Sean's DNA, so there was no point.

She typed: "How long can sperm live inside a woman?" *Up to five days. Longer in warm water.* She learned that if a man ejaculated in a tub and a woman was in the water, it was possible, unlikely, but possible, for sperm to migrate into the woman's body. So, it was possible, again, unlikely, but possible for a woman to get pregnant from a bath. She played with that idea for a while. She couldn't quite conceive of a situation in which a man would masturbate in a tub, then ejaculate, while the woman sat in it. But however it happened, it meant that a virgin pregnancy was actually possible. She wondered if it had ever happened. Of course no one would have believed the woman.

Men can leave genetic material other than sperm in women after sexual intercourse. She continued clicking. On a site of a spiritual nature she learned: *Every time a man ejaculates inside a woman, a part of him enters her, something more than sperm, something of the spirit.* Deidre believed that. She always felt energized after sex, as though with the sperm came some of the man's life force, while he, invariably, needed a nap, having lost some of his force.

She then clicked onto a medical site. *Male cells can be transferred to the female during intercourse.* Not just sperm, but cells. *These cells can be stored in the woman's body for years.* Deidre's body became electrified.

DNA tests on women had revealed the presence of male DNA. It occurred in women who had been pregnant with male fetuses, and strangely the DNA was most prominent in women who had aborted the male fetuses, rather than in those who had carried to full term. (She and Sean had always believed that their baby was a boy.) But it also occurred in women who had never been pregnant but had had intercourse. And it was possible for some of that genetic material to carry into future children. The scientific term for it was microchimerism. Her breathing became shallow.

She reread it to make sure she understood. "Oh my God," she murmured. She stared at the screen. Sean *had* managed to transfer and store some of his DNA in her. And she had transferred it to Seamus.

Deidre took deep breaths coaxing her body to quiet down and accept the truth. Sean was in Seamus. So, now it was time to make peace with everything—the abortion, her leaving him, his death, even her lingering love for him. She had to make peace so she could love Seamus without fear, without guilt. She had to accept him for who he was so she could raise him the way he should be raised. An image of him on ice skates invaded her thoughts. Yes, she would get him started on skates at three, the age Sean started skating. She began to feel an ease she hadn't felt in a long time.

When Phillip and Seamus came home, Seamus was ready for his nap.

They put him in together, watching as he let his eyes close.

"He really doesn't look like us, does he?" Phillip said once again.

Deidre smiled. "But he does. He looks a lot like us."

PURGE

She read that book and won't read it again, so it can go. And that one, too. This one, she'll never read. But she knows the author. He's only written one book and it's not that good. Still. Not everyone knows a published writer; that makes it worth keeping. This one, she started three times. But it was a gift from someone who still loves her. Does she throw it out because she doesn't love him? Put it in the laundry room of her building where someone might take it, start it, not finish it. Keep it for now—a reminder there's someone out there loving her.

All the ones about how to stoke creativity, even though the directive to be creative has become a burden—she just wants to watch Netflix at night and not feel guilty about how she isn't drawing or writing or knitting. But it's important to think about being creative. Keep them.

The yoga books—they were so expensive and she might go back to it again one day. But this is a purge, so choose one. *Restorative Yoga*—it never worked for her. And the *Yoga for Children* . . . had she ever imagined she'd teach yoga to children? So, toss. But then she is reminded of that visit to her sister's and the burning of yoga books in the firepit, along with her mysteries, romances and anything else that might be perceived as ungodly—a purge. An attempt to please God so he'd purge her of her illness. Does that change whether she should toss the yoga books? Toss the children's yoga; keep the restorative.

The books from her Freud phase and the mythology ones when she was trying to understand. Keep. But the self-help books . . . don't even look at the titles. Too pathetic. Toss.

The knickknacks on the bookshelves—the someone who loves her gave her the silver Buddha. Keep. The blown glass angel reminds her of her sister who believed in angels, whose book purge didn't purge her illness. The postcard of David Bowie in a duster-like belted coat. So cool, and she has wanted to be cool and she owns a coat similar to his and boots, too. And she bought them before she even had this postcard, so that suggests she was once pretty close to being cool. Plus, Bowie is dead now, too, and she likes seeing him, thinks of him every day.

All these flash drives. She'll check to see what's on them. But not today. So keep those.

Drawings from her daughter and little notes that are taped up on the shelves. Keep, of course. And the little wooden loon—keep because her daughter did a report on the common loon when she was in first grade, years ago, already.

In this little cloth sack—Life Savers, bobby pins. Toss. And Tums. Her belly always complaining. Toss—she has containers and containers of Tums.

In the closet—keep only the things that give you joy, Marie Kondo, the purge guru, says. None of it gives her joy. But this shirt, in particular, she hates. The fabric, the neckline. It seemed right in the store but never after that. Toss. But it was expensive. Toss. Yes, that feels good. She likes this blouse but it was a gift from her ex-husband; no, he's not the man who loves her. It's a beautiful bluish-green and she wears it on special occasions but he was often so harsh to her. Should she keep anything he gave her? Should she purge herself completely of him? Wouldn't that be healthy? But does she have to throw out a blouse she likes? Is she clinging to him if she clings to the blouse? Can't she just like it and wear it without it being about him? Keep it. Downgrade it to a work blouse, wear it until it means nothing.

These pants are uncomfortably tight at the waist. She washes her clothes too often, and yes, she has gained some weight. She eats healthy. She believes that. But she also eats frozen yogurt at night—sometimes the entire pint. And sometimes pretzels for dinner. Should she save the pants until she has something better to do at night than eat pints of frozen yogurt, until the waistband loosens. Toss.

The T-shirts. Rangers and Yankees—mementos of a time when she cared about sports. But . . . who won the World Series? Who won the Stanley Cup? And she hates the shape of T-shirts; never ever wears them. Toss.

Her sister's dress. It doesn't hold her smell. It used to. But it hasn't for years. Will she ever wear it? No, that would be too macabre, and besides it's so Little House on the Prairie. Don't make fun. Her sister liked it. It's pretty. It's been eight years since she died. Keep it.

Pick up the Yankees T-shirts from the pile. She loved the Yankees. She went to spring training with her best friend. She went to every home game for two seasons in a row with friends who were rabid fans and so much fun. They are more than T-shirts.

Leave the shoes for another time.

Her goal is to throw out twenty things. Twenty things and she can stop. She can feel less weighted down, less cluttered, less attached to material items, lighter, healthier. Cleansed. Joyful?

To her jewelry box. Some of the earrings actually make her happy. Joy? No. But she likes many of them. And her bracelets, too. So what that she rarely wears them. But these lapel pins her mother gave her . . . a silver-plated flower, a triangle, an arrow. Junk. Nothing she would ever wear. Nothing anyone would wear. Out. But her mother gave them to her and she has so little from her mother. And maybe her mother was trying. So keep the flower. Toss the arrow and the triangle. Her wedding ring.

Her engagement ring. Keep, of course. The gold crucifixes. The silver chains. No one throws real jewelry out. Toss the old receipts sitting in the bottom and move on.

Keep all the pills in the bathroom cabinet even though they're outdated. You never know. All the pain she endured, all the pain-killers she didn't take. Keep them. There may come a pain she can't endure or one she just doesn't want to endure. But the old eye drops—they can go. The expensive face cream, too expensive to use, now a café-au-lait color when it should be pearly white. Throw it out. Stop buying them. No, keep buying them. They give her hope--of what, she can't be sure. Maybe it's satisfaction and not hope but there's something about buying them, about applying them that makes her feel as if something good could happen. And imagine how bad she'd look if she didn't use a cream.

Her hair brushes. The brush for the wig. Just now she doesn't know why she kept it, how she could have kept it. Bad karma to have kept it? If her cancer were to come back, she would buy a new wig, buy a new brush for the new wig. Oh God, did she keep the wig? Talk about bad karma. Did she expect to have to wear it again? Is it in the back of a closet on a shelf? Hidden out of sight so as not to remind. But wouldn't she have thrown it out? It was expensive. But still. Throw out the brush. Forget the wig. Forget the cancer. No, find the wig and throw it out. Get on the step stool. Empty the closet shelves. Carry the step stool to the other closets. Gloves, hats, scarves. Get rid of all the hats. All of them. She never wears hats. Boxes of papers and cards. Another day. No wig. Thank God.

Take the piles and partial piles and get them out of the apart-ment. Then celebrate the purge with a glass of wine. But first a shower. A shower with the exfoliating gel and brush. No book burning for her but a scrubbing purge. Dry skin. Dead skin. Dead cells. Bad cells. Scrub. Pink skin. Tender skin. Raw skin. Purge the skin, now purge the blood. Like they did in the old days. Just a nick. A nick with one of the razor blades her husband left in the bathroom cabinet. She doesn't know why she kept them when she cleared out the rest of his things. But she's glad she didn't toss them because without them, she wouldn't be counting, one, two, three and then. . . the littlest nick. Just the thinnest line of blood, but a purge nonetheless. A letting-go of old blood. Bad blood. Sick blood. Not joy, but relief, release.

WALL MAN

The first time she noticed him, Kate thought she knew him. He had a vaguely familiar old neighborhood look—pale skin, faded brown hair that needed to be cut, Levi's jeans, a Rangers jacket; all the guys in her old neighborhood had been Rangers fans.

When he started appearing in her field of vision every day, leaning with one foot against the half-wall surrounding the garden apartment complex she passed on her way to drop off and pick up her seven-year-old twin girls at school, she assigned him a name—Wall Man—and a story. He was in his early fifties; he had no job, though he might have been one of those guys who had gotten started at ConEd at eighteen or nineteen, put in his twenty or twenty-five years and retired on a full pension, or more likely, someone who went out on disability; he lived in the garden apartments, which she knew were rentals—he didn't own; he was alone and lonely and had very little in his life except this wall. She realized she didn't know *him*, he just reminded her of people like him, people she tried not to think about, people like her brother Michael, with his small bachelor life that he was living out in the same room they had grown up in, with their mother who ate dinner with him in front of the TV watching *Wheel of Fortune.*

She told herself to ignore him.

"Watch out, Mommy!" shouted Jeanette, the older of the twins by two minutes and the nervous one. Kate hit the brake, just short of ramming the car in front of her.

"Who is he?" Jeanette asked.

"Who?"

"That man you were looking at."

"No one. I don't know. He just seems lonely. All alone like that."

"Who?" Jillian chimed in.

"No one. Just be grateful for everything and everyone you have. Not everyone has so much." Kate was actively practicing gratitude and teaching her girls to practice it, too.

"Thank you, Mommy," said Jeanette, ever anxious and anxious to please.

"Thank you," Jillian, the competitor, repeated.

In bed that night, Kate thought of telling her husband, Danny, about Wall Man, but then decided she didn't want to share him yet and didn't want to share the thoughts of her family he was triggering.

The last time Kate had seen her brother and mother, she went alone, having given them an ultimatum the visit before that she wouldn't bring the girls into that mess of a home. Her mother had begun hoarding glass bottles and jars and stuffed cats. The glass items, furry with dust, crammed the china cabinet and hutch, the side tables and the windowsills. Flies and gnats lay dead on the bottom of some, while the stuffed cats, hosting a legion of dust mites, Kate imagined, lay posed, peeking out a window, across the tops of chairs and the coach, in corners of the room, on the dining room table. The house smelled of decrepitude and garbage and deli meat, the odor of which wafted off Michael's clothes from his job at the neighborhood deli—a job he left when he was nineteen, only to return to at forty.

She thought the ultimatum was the kind of tough love they needed. She'd offered to help clean things up, pay for a cleaning service, rework Michael's resume. She'd suggested online sites and groups he could join to meet women. They both told her if she didn't like the house or them, she didn't ever have to come back. But she had given it another try. Nothing had improved. She tried not to have to use the bathroom when she visited—the toilet seat was one of those soft ones that hadn't been changed in years, the spigot in the sink was coated in toothpaste from Michael putting his lips over it to rinse his mouth. But on that last visit, she had drunk two cups of coffee before arriving—she wouldn't eat or drink anything there—and her bladder insisted. She passed her brother's room and looked in at the unmade bed, could smell the unwashed sheets from the doorway, saw the hand lotion on the edge of the bedstand and the magazines on the floor nearby—a naked girl on her widespread knees. Without wanting to, she pictured her brother lubricating his hand with the lotion and then yanking on himself while their mother sat in the living room stroking one of her cats. It wasn't the first time she thought they'd both be better off if they would just die. Smoke inhalation from a house fire. Carbon monoxide poisoning. Double suicide. Murder suicide. She couldn't imagine them being anything but abjectly unhappy. She prayed that God would put them out of their misery and in so doing, release her from the unrelenting responsibility she felt to rescue them. That had been over a year ago; she hadn't seen them since.

There he was again as she drove back from dropping the girls off at school. She tried to assign him a less dismal story as she passed. Maybe he didn't have a wife but he had a sister who was married and had children—four children—and they invited him up to their house somewhere in Putnam County or out on Long Island every weekend, and he was the favorite uncle who played football with the kids and gave them each a few dollars every time he saw them. And he was a history buff who watched the History Channel. And she gave him a cat, but then took it away, imagining a filthy, stuffed one.

But later, on the way back down the hill to pick up the girls, she looked over at Wall Man and couldn't make herself believe he had anything but that wall.

At dinner that night, Kate added a special prayer. "Bless those who are lonely and who don't have the nice life that we do, and show us the way to help them."

After the amen and the serving of the shepherd's pie, Danny asked about the added prayer.

"There's a man I see standing on the corner every day," she said. "I feel so sorry for him. He's all alone." Her voice quavered. "I wish there was something I could do."

Danny reached out to take her hand. "Is he an old man? Is he homeless?"

"No. He's older than us, but not old. And he's not homeless. He's just alone. He stands outside his building all day."

"You don't know that he's lonely. He may be perfectly happy."

"He reminds me of my brother."

Danny sighed. "Oh. Then maybe you should go see him."

"Maybe. But it's not just my brother. He's everyone who life was cruel to. It's hard to look at him."

"So don't look."

In bed that night, Kate thought about her brother and mother and how she moved on with her life and moved away from them, did better than they had, better than they had expected her to, how they resented her for it, calling her "The Queen" and calling the twins, "The Princesses" because she dressed well and dressed them well, asking if she thought having some money and a nice house made her better than them. But what was she supposed to have done? Stay in that house and live as miserably as they did? Bring them with her? She asked again for God to release them.

The next morning, she passed Wall Man on the way to school and decided she'd bake him a pie and give it to him on the way home with the girls. It was a small gesture, but it was something, and it would be good for the girls to see.

When she picked them up, she didn't tell them what she had in mind, only that the pie they were smelling in the front seat was for someone else. But as she drove up the hill, the pie began to seem like a paltry offering. How could a pie assuage his loneliness? And what would she say: I see you everyday; I thought you needed a pie?

She drove past, angry with herself for not having the courage to go through with the offering, frustrated that this was all she could come up with, and irritated at him for displaying his loneliness so obviously and unremittingly. Wasn't it just a little selfish of him to be out there advertising his plight every day, all day, with no concern for those who had to witness it?

At home, she was sorry she had blamed him for his suffering. But she realized she couldn't go on torturing herself over him. There was a simple solution—she could drive a different way to and from school and put Wall Man out of her sight and out of her mind.

The next day she went the other way, through a series of one-way streets, ending up well north of the school, and had to travel south on a street slow with lights and buses; she dropped the girls off several minutes late with Jeanette nearly in tears with worry. So, Kate decided she was being ridiculous; that he was only a man standing against a wall, and it was self-absorbed of her to feel that she couldn't face him.

Over the next two weeks, Kate tried to keep her eyes off him as she drove past, though she was always aware of him in the periphery. She donated to Operation Smile, and took on an extra child for Feed the Children. She gathered the clothes the girls had grown out of and then went to Target (quieting the voice that reminded her that if she'd been shopping for her own girls, she would have gone to Nordstrom's) and bought new hats, gloves, and socks and put them in a collection bin. She donated generously to the school's Thanksgiving food pantry collection. All of that made her feel a little better, but he was still there in her mind, standing against the wall, alone, and she was doing nothing to help *him*.

At night, in bed, she pictured him in his studio apartment, sleeping on a pullout couch. She wondered if he sometimes wandered out at night to his wall unable to sleep. She envisioned herself walking up and talking to him. He would be so glad for the company. And she would be generous; she would stand there with him for an hour or two. A relationship would develop. She enjoyed the stories of herself as rescuer and returned to them night after night. He invited her into his small apartment. They had coffee. He invited her again. She decided she wanted him to know the comfort of a woman, to know there was still love in the world, so she slept with him. She left her family and made a life with him. It was the ultimate sacrifice but Danny and the girls came to see it was the right thing.

In the mornings, she felt guilty and exhausted. She drank coffee until her hands trembled. After she dropped the girls off, she started going into the church, lighting a candle, and praying. She prayed for him to meet someone, prayed for him to move, prayed for God to take him out of his misery.

Too distracted to cook, she ordered pizza one night for dinner, then ordered it again the next day. For the rest of the week, she brought home a rotisserie chicken, a frozen lasagna, sandwiches from the deli. When Danny questioned her, she said she was tired and overwhelmed. She tried to explain that she had too much to do with the girls and the house, and at the same time, not enough. She was bored. She wasn't making a contribution in the world. Finally, she broke down and said she couldn't get Wall Man off her mind. "I feel like God is calling me to help him."

Danny asked if she wanted to go back to work.

She didn't, not while the girls were still so young. But she explained that she had a strong sense that she was supposed to do something.

The Thanksgiving break was coming, and it was their tradition to visit his parents in Florida. Danny booked a suite at a beachfront hotel with a pool and two restaurants. He urged her to make an appointment for a massage at the spa, and she did.

The massage relaxed her, as did sitting on the beach and looking out at the ocean; she felt peaceful for the first time in weeks. But at Danny's parents on Thanksgiving Day with the extravagant meal on the table and Danny's father saying the prayer, Wall Man surfaced in Kate's mind as if she had just driven around the corner and spotted him standing there, and she wondered if he were standing against the wall now, on Thanksgiving, if he had stood there all day waiting for the holiday to be over? And what had Michael and her mother done? Turkey heroes from the deli and bottles of Coke? She didn't want Danny to know that Wall Man was on her mind, so she smiled whenever he looked at her. But that night in bed, he said with some disappointment, "You've been thinking about him."

Her eyes welled up. "I feel so sorry for him."

"He's just some guy. He doesn't have anything to do with you."

"And my mother and brother," she cried.

Danny held her. "They have their lives. It may not seem like much to you, but it's what they have and what they want. They're happy with it. The same with the guy on the wall. He could be perfectly happy. You don't know. Stop feeling guilty. Stop thinking everyone's happiness is your responsibility."

When they returned home, she felt the tug of Wall Man but fought it. She went back to going the long way to school despite the fact that she was repeatedly late in getting the girls there. She forced herself to cook each night that week, even making her own pizza (store-bought crust) on Friday. She began to feel as though she was getting some control back in her life.

But that Sunday during the homily at Mass, Father Gupta spoke about the Advent season as a time for true generosity, of noticing the needs of others and performing acts of kindness. Kate felt as though he were speaking personally to her, as though he were telling her plainly that ignoring Wall Man was wrong. God expected more from her.

On Monday, she drove the long way to school. But on the way back, she drove up the hill. There he was. She responded with a strange sense of relief at seeing him there, followed by the familiar despair.

She lay awake again at night. In the morning, the darkness and the chill of the house hinted at the dreariness outside. She again went the long way to school—less hilly, safer in the freezing rain, but still, the roads were quite slippery. She drove back the long way, too, forcing herself to resist the Wall Man, promising herself a nap in her warm bed and then a hot latte from the new espresso maker Danny had bought as an early Christmas present. But once in front of the house, she couldn't get out of the car. She had to know if he was out in this weather.

The sleety rain let up and it was just drizzling, but the windshield wipers were crusted with ice and clearing only narrow arcs on the glass. She drove slowly, tapping the brake. She was thinking that she should invite her brother and mother for Christmas—an act of kindness, as Father Gupta had suggested.

She came down the hill, and there he was against the wall holding a black umbrella, spokes exposed on one side. She couldn't hold back the tears. She had to help him.

He was dead. Kate would recover—a broken collarbone, broken nose, bruises. The police questioned her in the hospital but were satisfied that it was an accident. She hadn't been on her phone, hadn't been under the influence of anything. The slippery road, the poor visibility, maybe a small patch of black ice were to blame. She must have lost control, they told her, and in a moment of confusion, hit the gas, hit the brake, hit them both, yanked on the steering wheel, jumped the curb. There would be no charges though the police warned her that the family might try to sue.

"Family?" she asked Danny when the police left her room.

"Kate . . . what happened? What did you do?"

"He had family?"

"The police said they were notifying his mother and his son. I think they said something about a sister, too. Kate, what happened? Tell me."

Kate closed her eyes, saw Wall Man through the windshield in her mind. Then she opened her eyes and looked at Danny and then the ceiling. She whispered, "He wasn't all alone."

"I know."

But she wasn't telling Danny; she was telling God.

HEAVENLY

The place is stuffy and yet quite cool. The exercise machines you spy in the gym on your way to a treatment room are old. Even from where you're standing, you can see the curling electrical tape on some of the seats.

You can't tell if the physical therapist who introduces himself as Dr. Munroe is wearing a wig; there's certainly something odd about his curly hair—too much of it up front, too much of it, in general, for a man his age. He instructs you to put on a gown. He wants to examine you and see the incision from the hip replacement.

The examination includes testing your leg's strength by having you lift it while he resists your efforts with his hand. You then bend your legs, stack your knees, and open them up. This is called clamshell. By now, the gown has crawled up to your waist and you're opening and closing your legs and showing him your crotch but you don't care because it's so difficult and you're beginning to feel nauseous and weepy with the effort. And you're disappointed and a little ashamed because you thought you were in good shape--before the surgery you exercised three times a week; practiced yoga, though not impressively; you're thin and relatively young for this—just forty-seven. But he tells you you're quite weak and very stiff. You begin to realize that you will not be the exception you thought you would be and the healing will take months, if not the full year the surgeon predicted.

You like Dr. Munroe, you decide. He seems to know what he's doing, and you can live with him seeing your underwear. When he is done examining you, he sends you into the gym, where the bored-looking assistant plays with her hair, hair which also looks a little unnatural (probably extensions). She helps you onto the old, small treadmill—no programs, just three buttons: on/off, speed, incline—and makes sure you're steady before she leaves to look at herself in the hallway mirror.

Over the next visits, you learn the routine: Dr. Munroe puts a heat pad and electrodes on your hip to simulate blood flow, which stimulates healing. After twenty minutes, he takes it off and makes you press your leg against his hand, and then do clamshells. On the third day, he brings in a board and a roller skate contraption and shows you how to "skate" with the one leg while you're lying down so the knee bends and the hip flexes; all the while, your underwear shows. (You only wear white cotton hipsters because if you wore something red or black or silky he might think you were sending him a message.) When you're done with the skating, he sends you to the gym where the assistant, whose name you learn is Kira, and who is studying to become a physical therapist, makes you walk on the treadmill and takes you out into the hallway where you can practice walking up and down steps. She even holds your hand. You wobble and waddle and still very much favor the good leg but you begin to see progress.

On your sixth or seventh visit, you arrive early and are taken into a room by a therapist whom you have seen in the office and are secretly a little afraid of. In a strong Eastern European accent, she introduces herself as Gertruda. "I will be your therapist for the day." Her therapy table is much neater than Dr. Munroe's. She has taken the time to fit the paper covering; there's a pillow at the head and a light blanket, which Dr. Munroe never offered, and on the table in a plastic wrapper is a pair of large paper shorts so that Gertruda can get to your hip without you having to expose your underwear entirely. You say, "Dr. Munroe never gave me shorts."

She says, "He never does, and he is not a doctor."

You can't help but notice that her blonde chin-length hair is obedient in an unnatural way and you start thinking of everyone in the office as the wig people. Gertruda wraps you with the moist heating pads and when you ask, expecting her to invoke an insurance prohibition, if she could please put one on your shoulder as it's been hurting—something to do with the way you put too much pressure on the cane—she tells you she noticed how high you were carrying that shoulder. She tells you that you should give up the cane and then she gets another pad and lays it horizontally across your shoulder. She covers you with the blanket, balances a bell on your chest, tells you to ring if you need anything, then turns out the lights and leaves you in peace.

The heat is so therapeutic and you're comfortable in a way you haven't been in a very long time. When Gertruda checks on you a little later, asking, "How is everything?" you want to reply descriptively and generously, so you sigh and say, "Heavenly." Gertruda repeats the word with the hint of a laugh. Mockery or appreciation? You hear her repeat it again as she closes the door. "She is finding the treatment 'heavenly.'" You decide she's mocking you. She's probably cocking her head in your direction, pulling her lips together, as though to say, *Get a load of this one.* You should have just said *nice.* Or even *lovely.* You have begun using the word lovely; even that feels a bit false in your mouth. But *heavenly*? It isn't in your vocabulary.

Soon the pad across your shoulder, which reaches to the exposed thin skin of your chest just below your collarbone, feels a little too hot. But you don't remove it. When the timer goes off, you don't ring the bell, thinking that it's rude to call someone with a bell; Gertruda will hear the timer, and if not, she'll have a sense of when the treatment is over. She does and is back in the room within three minutes of the timer going off. Still, she scolds you for not using the bell. And when she removes the pads and sees the red skin of your chest, she's angry. "You let yourself get burned? Why didn't you use the bell?"

You want to tell her that you aren't going to sue. That if that's her concern, she needn't worry. Instead, you lie, "It wasn't too hot. It felt good. It was nice." You are trying to take back the pretentiousness of *heavenly*, trying to replace it with words she won't resent you for: nice, good.

"Next time use the bell." She massages the scar on your hip, something Dr./Mr. Munroe never did, and she works you much harder than he did. You respond by working equally hard, fighting through your nausea, refusing to cry.

Gertruda is pleased. "I can see you want to work hard," she says. She also says, "You are my patient now. No more Mr. Munroe."

"Yes," you say, and you leave feeling stronger and thinking Gertruda likes you despite your vocabulary misstep.

There are words that belong to people and words that don't. You have a friend who can use the word *peevish* and though you like the word, if you used it, everyone you know would think you had heard someone else use it and then were stealing their word. *Lovely* might be your word. *Hideous* is definitely your word; you've used it enough times to make it yours. As you're limping to the bus stop, you realize that you have been hiding your range of vocabulary most of your adult life. You let it show in school because you were a pleaser and because you were generally afraid of your teachers, but you hid it with your friends, using profanity to demonstrate your expressiveness rather than any of the vocabulary words you easily memorized in class or learned from reading or from that period in your life when you read the dictionary. Because of that, you are, now, often at a loss for words; you have difficulty describing things accurately and when you try, as you did today, to be creative, you usually end up feeling stupid and like a fraud.

On the bus, you itch an irritated spot on your chest and think that you need psychological therapy; and you need a painkiller and some aloe vera.

At home, you take the painkiller and heat up some soup. You stupidly try to eat it while lying down on the couch and it dribbles onto your chest, burning the same spot that's already burned.

When you clean yourself up, you lie down again. You know you should be starting the new editing job your client sent but you need to rest. You also know that as a freelancer you should be looking for more jobs, but this guy sends enough for you to get by and your husband's job provides health insurance so you don't have that to worry about that. Or you didn't.

When he comes home, he wants to talk to you about The Separation. You've been talking about it for months, for years. You both have been holding onto the marriage for the sake of your son. You said you would stay together until he was in college. Now he's in college. You're not especially alarmed that your husband wants to talk about it, though you usually talk about it when you're fighting and the talking usually takes the form of yelling. But you haven't been fighting much lately. True, he's out more and you have been sleeping on the couch—it's just more comfortable on your hip—and you both know you can't recover the love you once had. But you can be companionable. And after all, he's the one who has the health benefits and the steady, somewhat impressive salary, so you haven't pushed the separation or the divorce because the fact is your body just isn't made for the stress of this life and it breaks down with regularity: sprains, migraines, carpal tunnel, irregular mammograms, a kidney infection, a bladder infection, winter eczema, allergies, dizzy spells, and now the hip. And no, you are not a hypochondriac. You would love to be strong like bull. You just aren't. So, you must have healthcare.

You begin unconsciously scratching the burn on your chest and he asks, "What's wrong?" when he really means what now?

You stop scratching.

Then he repeats, "I want to talk about the separation. Ethan is gone and I don't want to let this hip thing delay it."

You sit up as straight as you can manage. "This hip thing?"

"Don't get all upset."

"This hip has been bone on bone since I stopped growing, since I was eighteen. I've been in pain for years with this hip thing."

"Okay. Fine. I know. I'm sorry. But it's done now."

A question occurs to you. "Have you met someone?"

"No."

That is the answer you expected and expected to believe but now that he's said it, you're not so sure. You look at each other for a few moments, then you say, "I'm tired," and slouch back down and close your eyes until he leaves the room.

At your next appointment, Gertruda applies the heating pads but this time you say, almost apologetically, "Not here on my chest. I have a little rash."

She makes a quick face; she doesn't want to catch anything.

In fact, the rash has blistered, and though you know you shouldn't, you keep scratching it.

When you're all wrapped up and she's turned off the lights, she says, "Heavenly?" There's a wickedness to her voice or maybe it's just that you haven't had coffee and you have a headache.

"Nice," you say.

"Only nice? Not heavenly? What, I didn't do my job well today?"

You succumb. "It's heavenly."

Gertruda laughs a quick, "Ha." Then she adds, "So, off to heaven with you."

Off to heaven. Off to heaven. The words taunt you. You close your eyes to make them go away. You tell yourself that they're only words. Off to heaven. But they are words that feel like a curse. You knew it when you first said heavenly. A word that wasn't yours to use. A stolen word. And Gertruda knew, too, and she will make you pay for your transgression. "Off to heaven with you." You will get hit by a bus crossing the street . . . You tell yourself to stop before you go too far with this. "Stop." They are just words and just because Gertruda is Eastern European that doesn't mean she can conjure curses. These are the kinds of things your mind dreams up. You are a catastrophizer by nature. Gertruda has only given you an excuse. Off to heaven. Off to heaven. You scratch at your chest.

When Gertruda returns, you feel you must counter her curse, put your fingers into the shape of a cross to keep the evil back. Of course you don't do that. That's only a metaphor. But you say, as lightly as you can, "I'm not ready for heaven."

"Not ready for heaven?" She's puzzled.

"You said 'Off to heaven.' I'm not ready for heaven."

"Ah. But you said it was heavenly, no?"

"Yes."

"So."

You think about making your next appointment with Dr./Mr. Munroe but there's the underwear thing and you don't want to be silly. It isn't a curse. The heat really is heavenly. She works you hard again and you're making progress. Gertruda is a good therapist and you want to heal, so you make your next appointment with her.

On the way to the bus, you turn your ankle on uneven pavement but you do not fall. Gertruda has been urging you to give up the cane but you have not given it up and without it you would have fallen. You feel vindicated, powerful over her curse.

By the time you get home, everything hurts—head, hip, shoulder, ankle. You take a painkiller and understand why people get addicted: they make you feel lovely (yes, lovely is one of your words), not just pain-free, which is miraculous, but youthful and fluid and peaceful. When your husband comes home and brings up the separation again, you smile. "We don't have to resolve this tonight, do we?" When he says, "Yes," your peacefulness holds. It isn't until he tells you that he has already found a new place for himself that you can appropriately rile yourself up. You yell, you cry. He reminds you that you wanted this, too, that in fact, you were the first one to bring it up years ago. That's probably true, but lately you've come to believe that the two of you would never actually formally split up. You would lead separate lives but you would find a way to be comfortable roommates. After some years, you might buy a small summerhouse or condo and one of you would spend more time there than the other. There would be no need for a divorce.

It's only a separation, your soon-to-be husband-in-absentia tries to assure you, not a divorce, so you will remain on his health-care plan, and he will continue making the mortgage payments on the co-op; you will have to pick up the maintenance. But at some point, he says, the two of you will have to sell the co-op, unless you can buy him out. He tries to reassure you again by saying that won't happen for a while. He's gone within a week.

Though you've always done most of the cleaning and cooking, it quickly becomes overwhelming and unnecessary. Why bother with any real cooking when you're the only one eating and you don't care that much about food, anyway. So you eat popcorn for dinner, supplementing with frozen yogurt for protein; sometimes you eat a floret of raw broccoli, a superfood. You don't call anyone and no one calls you. Right after the surgery, people called but no one has called in days. It's your own fault. You don't keep in touch; you don't reach out to people. You generally like to be left alone. You realize that Gertruda is the person you see most, the person you speak to most. This depresses you more than you are already depressed, and it makes you angry at Gertruda. You would like to cancel your next appointment because it's pathetic that your physical therapist is the person you are closest to and because you just don't want to leave the apartment. But you're still something of a pleaser, and not showing up would displease Gertruda, so you go.

"Off to heaven with you."

At night, you lie awake listening for every sound. A mouse? A rapist? You think you smell gas. You scratch at your chest.

After a few visits, Gertruda notices that you're not working as hard as you used to and that you've lost some weight and look tired. You have no defenses, no energy for guile, so you say, "My husband left me." Then you revise. "We split up."

She nods. "Ah."

You're sure she disapproves; you're sure her husband would never leave her. She's probably been married for forty-five years, though she looks only to be in her late-fifties. To your surprise, she says, "I left a husband. I had my two daughters but I left." Hers is going to be a story of heroism, you can tell, unlike yours. "He wouldn't work and I wouldn't have it. I took my daughters and that was all."

"It must have been hard."

"What is hard? Everything is hard. I worked. I cooked. I cleaned. What can I do? I have to do it." She wraps you in the heat. "Now, I have a good husband."

"You remarried."

"I did. A hard worker, like me. And now I am happy."

"That's good."

Gertruda smiles. "Is very good." Then she asks, "Do you work? Is very important to work."

You assure her that you work, though you have a draft of a personnel manual on your computer that you're supposed to be proofreading and editing and that you are behind on.

"And here, too," she says. "You must work here. This is no place for laziness."

You stiffen when she turns off the light.

"Off to heaven with you."

Before you leave, she instructs you, again, to give up the cane. You say, "Yes," but won't do it. She says that you're getting psychologically dependent on it. This is true. You have begun to love your cane. You sleep with it at night so that you can grab it if you need to rush out of the apartment, hit an intruder across the head, get to the bathroom without falling, so that you can feel something up against you, even if it's stingily thin.

Your apartment has started to smell because you've locked all the windows. You used to always leave the windows open and your home never smelled. But you live on the second floor and someone could scale the walls. You have to think about your safety now that you are alone. But you don't like the smell. It makes you feel as though you live in an old lady's apartment. It makes you feel as though you are aging at an accelerated rate even though the hip replacement was supposed to make you feel youthful.

You decide you need more than painkillers, maybe antidepressants. Or sleeping pills. Yes, if you could sleep, you might not be so depressed, might not be so anxious. You might be able to open a window without worrying. So, you get yourself to your internist, looking your worst—no makeup, dark circles, a baggy shirt—in other words, what has become your usual. You tell him about the separation, tell him you haven't slept. You need to sleep to keep your strength up for the PT. He suggests counseling and you agree that you need that but for now you must focus on the PT and on sleeping. You lie to him and say that you're not taking any painkillers; no need to worry about overdosing on pain pills and sleeping pills. He concedes and gives you a prescription. Because you feel like you're getting away with something, you want to get out of the office quickly, so you don't bother to show him the sore on your chest that has been oozing.

Before your next appointment with Gertruda, the PT office calls and says the insurance hasn't paid for the last two visits. They will likely pay, the receptionist says, but she's obliged to tell you that if they don't, you'll have to pay out of pocket for those two sessions and any future sessions. You ask her if you should cancel your sessions until the issue is straightened out and she says that's the best course of action.

With no schedule whatsoever to keep, you feel giddily free, and that first night you stay up as long as you want to not worrying about when you will sleep. You keep thinking that you may even put in some time on the personnel manual or get up and do some organizing and dusting but you stay on the couch watching TV. At 2 a.m., you take your sleeping pill.

A few days later, the PT office calls; the insurance issue is resolved. But you don't feel so well. Your hip has been hurting in a way that's new to you, and a little scary. It throbs and is tender when you lie on it and is slightly warm to the touch. The scar seems a little redder than usual but you can't be sure. You've had chills and it's likely you have a fever, so you tell yourself and the receptionist that you have the flu. She kindly tells you to rest and drink fluids.

You resolve to return to PT when you feel better, to start cooking again, to call your client and tell him what you've been going through and promise to finish the manual by next week. You will clean the apartment. You will wear makeup. You will use your vocabulary. You will give up the cane. And you will stop wallowing. Your husband didn't leave you; the two of you split up. It's what you wanted.

For now, you lie on the couch scratching your chest, realizing that it's probably infected. It occurs to you that your hip might be, too, that some infection from your chest might have travelled to your hip. Infection is the thing to be avoided at all costs. It could become massive and resistant, destroy the replacement. You should be on an antibiotic. You will call the doctor but not now because the pain is finally dulling, after three or was it four painkillers. And the sleeping pills you took are kicking in. The peacefulness comes over you. Everything will be fine. You smile as you close your eyes. It's more than peaceful. It's heavenly. Off to heaven with you.

SEEKING GRACE

Lori and Eric Briggs sat on Patricia Palmieri's couch being pawed and nosed by her dog.

"Pet him," Lori whispered to Eric.

Eric obliged. "Good dog." To Lori he whispered, "He's a nutjob."

"Shh."

"I'll be right there," Patricia, director of Bright Light Adoption Agency, called from a bedroom she turned into an office. "Just making copies. Is Petey bothering you?"

"Not at all," Lori called back.

Petey began humping Eric's leg.

"Oh shit. Get off. Get off me, you horny bastard." Eric tried to shake Petey off.

"Just another minute," Patricia said.

"No rush," Lori replied.

Eric mumbled, "We've only been waiting a year and a half. So, yeah, no rush." He pried Petey from his leg and gave him a firm push with his foot.

"Please shut up."

"It's not like she'll take the baby away from us."

"I know. But please. This whole thing . . . this dog . . . this apartment . . . her keeping us waiting. It's all freaking me out."

Finally, Patricia entered the room waving a thick Express Mail envelope. "Sorry about that. Here she is." She handed the packet to Lori, and Eric took hold of her wrist as if the packet were so heavy she needed his support to steady it.

"Let me get Petey out of here." She took him by his collar, directed him into the office/bedroom, closed the door, then, as he scratched, said, "He'll be okay," as if Lori and Eric were concerned.

"So," Patricia sat on a chair and leaned forward. "Ready?"

Lori took a breath. "Ready."

"Let's meet your baby."

Later, in the car, Lori scrutinized the photographs: one headshot, and one casual pose of the baby in a walker. "I'll bet this was the only time she was in a walker. Look," Lori observed, "she's just propped in it; she doesn't even look like she can sit up, never mind walk."

"I don't like that picture," Eric admitted. "She's scowling."

Lori studied it. "She looks pissed. Look at her little furrowed brow. I like that she knows enough to be angry. She's in an orphanage; she should be angry."

"I like the headshot. The first one we saw. She looks so innocent."

"I don't like that one as much."

"No kidding. You didn't say a word when you turned over the cover sheet and saw it. What were you thinking?"

Lori hesitated. "Honestly? I guess I was thinking she looks Chinese."

Eric laughed. "I thought that, too."

"It wasn't that I was shocked," Lori explained. "Obviously, we knew she was Chinese. I guess it's just that it's been so abstract until now." She paused. "And I just didn't get a feel for her from that first photo. Her head is kind of floppy and she has no expression on her face."

"I fell in love with her as soon as I saw her," Eric asserted.

Lori couldn't help but feel a little resentful. They had discussed this on the way to Patricia's apartment and several times before that. Lori had wondered when they would fall in love with their baby. Would it be as soon as they saw the photo, or later, in China, when they held her in their arms? She had reminded Eric of the difficult truth a friend had admitted after giving birth. This woman knew she was supposed to love her baby and she wanted to, but it didn't happen the moment she held him, and she felt betrayed by all the claims of spontaneous motherly love she had heard about. With that story, Lori prepared herself for the possibility of a developing love rather than an instantaneous one, though she hoped for the latter. She and Eric had also talked about how carefully they would record the process of the adoption and the baby's early history with them because there'd be little or no recorded history of her infancy—of her time with her birth mother and her months in the orphanage— and now as Lori considered Eric's pronouncement, she decided that he might just be saying that he fell in love on sight because he wanted that to be part of his story about his little girl, what he'd tell her years later when they talked about her adoption. It had been his idea to keep a journal—a memory book—one in which he and Lori would write side-by-side entries. *I loved you at first sight*, would be Eric's first entry. And that was the way it should be, Lori conceded. Whether he really fell in love with her at first sight didn't matter; he had made it true by saying it.

"I'm in love, too," Lori said. But seeing the baby's photographs hadn't resolved the uneasiness that had been plaguing her for the past few weeks. She had tried to articulate it to Eric by saying that she felt like she wanted to crawl out of her skin. She feared she was having a nervous breakdown. Eric dismissed it all with, "It's the adoption and the anticipation of motherhood," as if Lori somehow might have overlooked that.

But it wasn't the adoption because, for one thing, Lori wasn't overly anxious about it. At first, she had been ambivalent; by the time she met Eric, she was thirty-six and had gotten used to the idea that she might not have children. She had gone through her period of feverishly desiring them, going so far as to indulge in a few contraceptiveless nights with boyfriends she knew she wouldn't stay with. But after a while, the wanting dissipated, and though she would have liked the companionship of a husband, she began to appreciate the childless indulgences of her life: sleeping late on weekend mornings, the drawing classes and other classes she took for free at the Y where she was an assistant director, staying late when she wanted to attend events, the art supplies and books that she spent too much money on, her long work-outs, long walks, long baths, her skimpy meals. But Eric, three years younger and a Phys Ed teacher, surprised her with his enthusiasm for marriage and kids, and convinced her that not so deep down in her protected heart, she still wanted children. Certainly, she could remember wanting them, so it was easy to believe him. Her body, though, was not so willing to be persuaded; it resisted pregnancy for the first three years of their marriage, then finally cooperated only to later reject the fetus. There were months and months of trying again, then another miscarriage, and as Lori turned forty-two, she began to console herself again with the memory of not wanting children.

But then there was that little Chinese girl who looked back at Lori and Eric and waved as she crossed the street, and her mother who took her hand and hurried her across—her blonde-haired mother—and before Eric and Lori reached the other side of the street, one of them—Lori remembers it being her, Eric remembers it being him—had asked, "Would you ever think about adopting?" A cautious wanting poked up in her again, and the more they explored it, the less cautious her wanting became because this time the wanting was independent of her body. This time, her body could not fail her.

Once they had decided, they became relieved at leaving reproduction behind and made a joke of being rescued from their genetics: deafness on his side of the family in a second cousin, diabetes and a bipolar aunt on hers. Big ears and big feet on both. They recalled how they had always intended to do something significant, how they both always intended to help. With the adoption, they'd finally be doing something. They chose an adoption agency, struggled with the paperwork, argued over who was doing more than the other, complained about the maddening multitude of forms, were almost defeated by it, but finally completed all of it. Then they waited and some of the forms expired and had to be redone. And they waited some more. And after a year and a half, when they thought they couldn't bear another week of waiting, Patricia called saying she had their referral—they had been assigned a baby.

Lori sat in the car looking at the photos of the baby, trying to conjure a sense of motherhood. She told herself that it was natural that she didn't feel like the baby's mother yet; the referral was only photos and measurements. When she actually held the baby's thirteen pounds, twenty-five inches in her arms, she'd swoon.

"It still doesn't feel real," she said.

"I want to go and get a journal now," Eric said, fatherhood clearly real for him. "I want a good one. One of those leather-covered ones. Not red. I don't want her to think that because she's Chinese, everything has to be red. And we'll stop and make copies of the photos so we can start sending them to people."

"I don't want to send the headshot," Lori said.

"I don't know why you don't like that one. She's beautiful."

"I'm not telling you which one to like. Don't tell me."

"Fine. Send the one of her scowling to your family. I'm sending the headshot to mine." Excited, he continued, "I love her name. Meilin. It's beautiful."

"It is," Lori agreed. "We'll keep it as her middle name. Grace Meilin." They had decided on Grace—a compromise for both of them. Lori wanted Julia. Eric wanted LeeAnn. But they both had come to like "Grace."

Lori envied him his joy; at the same time, she felt betrayed by him for having such intense feelings without her. She looked out the window, wondering what was wrong with her.

Several days later when she was "whipping around," as Eric called her recent restless flipping from side to side in bed, Lori pushed the pillows away, lay on her belly and detected a tenderness in her breasts. She tried to attribute it to the exercising she had done earlier, but the panic-like electricity that shot through her alerted her that incline presses at the gym were not the cause of the soreness. After a fitful night, she showered, left the house without taking the time to put on makeup, stopped at a drugstore, and when she got to work, went straight to the restroom. She chose the disabled person's stall because of its roominess, opened the pregnancy test, urinated on the stick and stared at it until an urgent plus sign surfaced in the panel. She sat back on the toilet, stunned, yet not surprised, until someone entered the ladies' room and Lori roused herself, wrapped the stick in toilet paper, threw it out, washed her hands, glanced wide-eyed at herself in the mirror, felt tears coming on and retreated back into the stall until the other woman left. Lori emerged, splashed water on her face, put a wet paper towel to the back of her neck and prepared herself to tell her boss that she was going home sick.

After Lori called Eric, he left work early, too, and came home looking like a proud expectant father. "I know exactly when this happened," he claimed. "You were crying because we hadn't gotten the referral yet. We made love. Remember that night?"

"What are we going to do?"

"What can we do? We'll have two kids. Grace Meilin will have a sister. Or a brother. It's better for her not to be an only child, anyway. And now I get to see a little you running around."

"I don't want to see a little me running around," Lori cried. "Or a little you. I don't want to be pregnant now. We're going to China. And I don't want to go through another miscarriage. I can't believe this." She shrugged Eric off when he put an arm over her shoulder in an attempt to calm her. "The only good thing about this is that now I know what's been wrong with me. You kept saying I was nervous over the adoption. It wasn't the adoption."

"But it was motherhood. I said 'motherhood,' too." Eric smiled, trying to humor her.

"It's not funny. I thought I was having a breakdown. I knew something was wrong. This is pretty telling—pregnancy feels like a breakdown."

Two days later, Eric and Lori were in the obstetrician's office watching a monitor as the doctor pointed out the twinkling star that was the baby's heartbeat.

"I can't tell you how many times I've heard this," Dr. Dibray said. "A couple decides to adopt and then gets pregnant."

"I never heard of it," Lori retorted.

"Well, now you have," Dr. Dibray answered.

"What are the chances that I'll miscarry, again," Lori asked bluntly.

"Let's take this week by week," the doctor suggested.

"What about the traveling? Is it safe for her to travel?" Eric asked. "We're on our way to China in a few weeks."

"I don't advise it, frankly. These are critical weeks. You'll have to be very careful." She shook her head for emphasis. "Stay away from the water, for one thing. You can't risk getting a parasite. You did get your hepatitis shots, right?"

"I did," Lori answered.

"Do you know anything about the medical care over there?"

"Not really."

"Well, you better find out. Just in case. See if you can get an English-speaking doctor, at least. And with your history, you should be off your feet as much as possible. Absolutely no straining. No lifting. Nothing strenuous. Okay? You've got to do whatever you can to help this one along."

Lori nodded. Outside the office, she cried.

"This always happens," Patricia laughed when Lori called later to ask about medical facilities in China.

"That's what my doctor said," Lori responded, unamused.

"I had one woman who came back from China with a daughter and then got pregnant with twins."

"Oh, God," Lori moaned. "I can't even wrap my mind around the idea of two kids."

Patricia informed her that there were American medical centers in China, though not one in the province they'd be staying in. She did admit that it wouldn't be that easy to get to it. She also advised Lori not to mention the pregnancy while in China unless there was an emergency. "This changes your application. The Chinese officials would have to reassess all your financial statements and your home-study with two children in mind. It probably wouldn't matter, but we don't want to take any chances." She paused. "You must be overwhelmed."

"I am."

"You know you can think about putting the adoption off for a few weeks if you need to. We have to get an appointment at the American Consulate for the baby's visa and then you plan the trip around that, as you know—but we could just not apply for the Consulate date now. We could wait until the next group of referrals comes in and you would travel with those people. That would give you another month or so. Meilin would stay assigned to you. You'd just go and get her a little later. Would that help?"

"Really? Is that a possibility?" Lori felt some relief, immediately followed by guilt. "But I don't want to leave her there."

"She'll be fine. It's not ideal, I know, but I'm telling you, this kind of thing happens all the time and people have no choice but to postpone. Someone once got pregnant right after she handed in her paperwork and ended up due to deliver at the same time she was supposed to be in China. People get sick at the last minute, someone in the family dies. Things happen. If you need to take some time, regroup, you can. I'm not pushing you. Just think about it."

"Thank you. I will."

"How is waiting going to help?" Eric enquired when Lori presented Patricia's proposal while they sat at the kitchen table.

"I'm not sure. But if I'm going to miscarry, maybe it'll happen by then. I don't want to miscarry over there."

Eric shook his head. "So, now we have to hope that you'll miscarry in the next few weeks?"

"I don't know what we're supposed to hope for," Lori answered impatiently.

"What happens to Meilin if we wait?"

"Nothing, according to Patricia. She's still ours."

"Is that what you want to do?"

"It's not what I want to do," Lori answered. "I can't stand the idea of leaving her in the orphanage for another few weeks. But if I'm going to miscarry, and you know there's a good chance of that, I want to do it here. I hemorrhaged the last time. But leaving Meilin in the orphanage is not what I want to do, so don't ask me like that."

Eric defended himself. "I'm just trying to figure this out."

"I'm trying to figure this out, too," Lori snapped.

They sat silently, each looking away from the other. Then Eric asked, "When did the last miscarriage happen?"

Lori glared at him. She drew her eyebrows together in a question, finding it both offensive and hard to believe that he could have forgotten. It was on Halloween, two years before. "Trick or treat?" she reminded him.

"No. I know when it happened," he clarified. "I meant how many weeks along were you?"

Without hesitation she remembered, "I was in my eleventh week. I'm seven weeks now. Four weeks away."

"What about the one before that?"

"Later. Around the fourteenth week."

"So, seven weeks away. Should we wait past the fourteenth week, too?"

"I don't know. I don't know if we could postpone that long." Lori shook her head. "A pregnancy should be good news."

Eric sighed. "It is good news." He repeated, "It is," as if he were trying to convince them both.

The next day, with Lori sitting across the room from him, Eric called Patricia (*Please*, Lori had pleaded, *I can't face her*) and told her to delay their trip.

The next weeks marked themselves for Lori with a loss of appetite and energy; morning sickness that lingered into early evening; an episode of spotting, which unnerved her despite her ambivalence about whether she wanted this baby. Because they didn't know what they should hope for, they spoke about Lori's pregnancy but said very little about the baby growing inside her and even less about Meilin.

Patricia called to reassure them (and remind them, Lori couldn't help thinking, as if they could possibly forget) that Meilin was still theirs. The next time she called it was to tell them that the group they were to have originally traveled with was in China and had been united with their babies and all had gone well. She had thoughtfully asked one of the families to take a picture of Meilin for Lori and Eric but the orphanage director had refused this request. "Policy," Patricia said. But Lori knew as well as Patricia did that it was a policy he had made up on the spot perhaps to show his displeasure with the delinquent parents-to-be, perhaps to remind them of his power over Meilin's destiny. That night, Lori lay awake in bed facing away from Eric, imagining what it would have felt like to have Meilin placed in her arms, imagining that Eric was picturing the same thing.

In the eleventh week of the pregnancy, Lori became even more acutely aware of her body, of any sign that the fetus was letting go. She had done her best not to attach herself emotionally to this baby, though she had begun to take care of it in small ways—putting her feet up at the end of the day, making sure not to carry heavy packages. More than once, she stood sideways at the mirror trying to imagine herself at nine months.

"We're in the eleventh week," she reported cautiously to Eric. "I know."

A few days later, Patricia left a message saying that the next set of referrals had come in, and she was beginning to schedule dates at the Consulate. She wanted to know if they were ready for her to schedule theirs.

Lori played the message for Eric when he got home that evening. He listened, and for several minutes, neither of them said anything. Then surrendering to the sentence that had been uttering itself in her head for weeks, Lori blurted, "I don't think I can go to China."

Eric sighed, sat down on the couch, clasped his hands behind his head, and stretched his neck to either side. "I've been thinking of that, too," he finally admitted. "The flight will be a real strain on you. We have to switch planes twice going and three times coming back. You have to worry about the water once we're there. Besides that, I don't know what you'd eat. You don't like Chinese food. What if you get sick? Plus you can't carry Meilin. The doctor said no lifting. You can't even carry a suitcase."

"I know." There were more reasons but Lori tried not to seem in a hurry to present them. "Plus there's all the internal travel," she began haltingly. "The car ride from Shanghai to Nanjing. Patricia says that's harrowing. They drive like lunatics. Then there's the long bus trip to the orphanage and back to the hotel."

Eric added, "Then we have the flight from Nanjing to the consulate in Guangzhou. Plus, it's winter. It'll be cold and wet." He kneaded the muscles at the base of his neck.

"It's not just the trip," Lori sat down. "Because if it were, you could go alone, I guess. I don't know if that would mean more paperwork. I don't even know if we'd have that as an option at this point. But if we did, when we got her home, you'd have to go right back to work, and I'd be alone with her. I'm not supposed to pick her up. I'm supposed to be off my feet. But she'll need to be carried; she should be held all the time so she can bond."

"I know."

"I guess I could just lie in bed with her," Lori mused, unpersuasively.

"No, she'll need stimulation. She'll need to play and be outside." He shook his head. "Do you have any sense of . . . I mean," he hesitated, "how does the pregnancy feel?"

"Are you asking me whether or not I'll miscarry? Don't you think I wish I knew?"

"I just don't know what to do," Eric got up, walked to the window then walked back and stood in front of Lori. "Why is this such a mess? Why couldn't this happen when we wanted it to happen?"

Crying, Lori answered, "I don't know."

Eric sighed, steadying himself. "Don't cry." He sat down again and put an arm around Lori. "We wanted a baby, right? A biological baby? I didn't want it to be this complicated but I wanted to have a baby with you. So, we should be happy about that. Right? Why can't we be happy about that?"

"What about Meilin?" Lori asked.

Eric shook his head again. "I don't know. But I don't see how we do this. I think we have to call Patricia and tell her we can't go. Right? I mean . . . you definitely shouldn't go, and I can't do it on my own. We have to ask what would happen if we didn't adopt her, ask her if she would be adopted by someone else."

"Oh God. This is unbelievable." Lori looked at Eric. "She was already abandoned once. Now, we're doing it to her, too? And what if we give her up, and then I lose this baby."

Eric was silent for a few moments. "Then we have nothing."

It was Eric, again, who made the call to Patricia. She coolly told him that Meilin would be made available to another family; she'd try to get her assigned quickly. That evening just before she sat down to dinner, Lori hesitantly removed the photos of Meilin from the refrigerator.

"Don't you think I should?" she asked when Eric stopped eating to watch her.

"Give me them," he said. He took the photos and kissed each one, even the one of Meilin scowling. Then Lori kissed them, too, and hugged them to her chest. When she placed the photos in the accordion folder marked "adoption," she felt as though she were putting Meilin in the grave.

She was glad she and Eric hadn't found a journal either of them liked the evening they made copies of Meilin's photographs. A single entry made that night in an otherwise blank book would be too vivid an illustration of how abruptly they had turned their backs on her. She was also relieved not to have to reread anything she would have struggled to write that night. She loved Meilin at first sight, she believed now; but she had protected herself from that love which she instinctively sensed she would lose. She envied Eric that he hadn't known to protect himself, and she regretted having missed the opportunity to experience the pure joy that he had felt in those first days of their acquaintance with Meilin.

The fourteenth, fifteenth, and sixteenth weeks passed. Lori left her job and stayed off her feet as much as she could. *Please,* she began to whisper to the baby, as she lay on the couch, *please let me be your mama.* In the twentieth week, with the amniocentesis behind her, Down syndrome and Fragile X ruled out, the gender confirmed—a girl (maybe a conciliation for Meilin, Lori thought)—she felt the baby kick.

"This one is going to make it," she said to Eric one night. "We should think of names."

"Shh," he told her, "don't jinx it."

In her thirtieth week, Lori called Patricia. Everyday Lori worried about whether Meilin would really be adopted by someone else or if she would become one of those ten-year-old girls she and Eric had seen on the DVD that Patricia had taken the last time she visited orphanages—ten-year-old girls who had once been babies, but who, for whatever reason, had not been designated as adoptable, or designated but never assigned to a family. Or worse, designated, assigned, then refused by the prospective parents. They had looked into Patricia's camera and knew there would be no family for them. "I just need to know that she's all right," Lori said, and in the pause that followed, she couldn't help launching into a reiteration of the reasons for their decision, realizing as she was making what must have sounded like excuses, that Patricia must distain her for seeking absolution.

But Patricia was merciful and professional. "Don't worry," she assured Lori. Meilin is fine."

"Is she being adopted?" Patricia hesitated. "Information about adoptions is confidential. But I'll put it this way. I expect to meet her at the annual agency picnic in August."

"Really? So she's home with someone or will be home soon?"

"That's all I can tell you. The family has a right to their privacy."

"Of course. I . . . I'm just so happy for Meilin. I'm happy for those parents."

"And how are you?" Patricia asked almost as an afterthought. "Did you have your baby yet?"

"Another few weeks."

"Well, good luck."

After she hung up, Lori went onto the agency's website and noted the date and place of the annual picnic. Over dinner that night, Lori cautiously mentioned the news about Meilin, aware that her name, which had not been spoken between them for weeks, was an abyss she and Eric were still falling into.

"We should be happy for her," she remarked when Eric took the news silently. When he continued in his silence, she got up and began clearing the dishes.

In her thirty-fifth week, Lori lost three pounds. The doctor didn't seem especially alarmed and told her to just keep eating. On Tuesday of the following week, Lori realized the baby had stopped moving.

She made an emergency appointment, and Dr. Dibray immediately put her on the sonogram. Lori watched as the baby came into focus. It was like looking at her in a deep part of the ocean, except that where there should have been eternal motion, nothing even swayed. Lori closed her eyes and tried to breathe life into the stillness.

"Ah, here we are," Dr. Dibray said, as though she knew all along she would find what she was looking for.

When Lori opened her eyes and saw the light that was the baby's heart flickering on the screen, she wept as though the news were bad, her relief triggering grief for all the babies she had lost.

Dr. Dibray scheduled a Caesarean section for later that day. As Eric drove to the hospital, Lori whispered, "Please. Please."

Once they were in the room with Lori lying safely on a bed, hospital staff nearby, Eric tried to distract her from her nervousness. "Well, I guess now we can start thinking about names."

They both knew it wouldn't be Grace.

"I like Daisy," Lori said. Not a name from any of the lists they had made when they were thinking of an American name for their Chinese baby.

"Daisy?"

"Yeah. It's cute. I want to name her after a flower. Something sweet and simple." She looked at him, wanting him to understand that she couldn't bear to name this baby anything as spiritual or hopeful as 'Grace.'

"I like it." He smiled, wanly.

When the doctor arrived, Lori said tentatively, "This is really going to happen."

"Yes, it is," the doctor answered.

After the delivery, Dr. Dibray explained that Lori's placenta had failed. "She hasn't been getting much nourishment," she said of the baby. "She'll be hungry."

And when she could take her to her breast, the baby latched on with such ferocity that Lori yelped.

"I love her," she told Eric, crying. "I loved her all along."

Neither Eric nor Lori thought to have their names removed from the adoption agency's mailing list, and when the newsletter came, Lori thought, at first, she would throw it away, protect them from the guilt it would recall. But she was ashamed of the silence around Meilin, ashamed they had become cowards who couldn't talk about the baby they left behind. Plus, she was curious.

The newsletter featured a short article about adoption from a father's perspective; a travel checklist that Lori remembered from the newsletter the year before: gifts for the orphanage caretakers, outfits and toys for the babies, dossier and copies of the dossier, drugstore items for all the conditions the baby might have. And on another page was the news she both hoped for and dreaded: a list of families and babies recently returned from China. She glanced quickly over the first names—*Sophia, Lily, Lucy, Maya*—but it was the middle names she sought, hoping that the parents would have preserved her Chinese name that way. Her eyes dropped to it. *Meilin. Anna Meilin.* Her heart leapt. For a moment, she was Lori's and Lori was the mother of two daughters, and she thought, just fleetingly, *I could have done it.* But she corrected herself. No, she couldn't have and her mind registered the rest of the entry: *Anna Meilin Giordana. Daughter of Anne and Anthony, New Jersey.* She wasn't Lori's. She was Anne and Anthony Giordana's, Anne and Anthony who had gone to China and brought Meilin home.

She left the newsletter on the table with the magazines and newspapers. If Eric saw it, he didn't mention it.

A few nights later, after they had put Daisy to bed for the second time—she slept in two-hour increments—Eric and Lori foraged in the refrigerator and cupboards for snacks and then returned to the living room to watch TV and nap before the next round of waking. As Eric flipped stations, Lori said, "Meilin is home."

Eric only nodded.

Lori didn't know what she expected to find when she drove to the adoption agency picnic. Would she look for Meilin? Look for Patricia and show her Daisy, proof that not going to China had been a necessary decision. When she arrived, she realized she could do nothing but sit on the outskirts of the picnic and watch the families with their little Chinese girls.

She was not surprised when she looked up and saw Eric. In fact, she was relieved, as though she had been waiting for him, as though she hoped he would find her there. When he saw her, he cocked his head and smiled, glad to see her, glad to see that it was okay that he had come looking. Lori patted the bench as though she had been holding that spot for him. Eric sat down, kissed her, kissed Daisy, then said quietly, "I thought I could find her."

"I know," Lori whispered. They would spend the rest of their lives wondering, sending their souls and sometimes their bodies out seeking.

Eric shook his head then leaned into her.

They blinked tears onto Daisy's blanket, then after a few moments, they smiled tenderly at each other, kissed, then turned to look out onto the field of black-haired babies.

A HEAVEN OF THEIR CHOOSING

Liz Kiely and her mother, Gail, were having dinner on the terrace of Gail's co-op when the phone rang.

"It's John," Gail mouthed.

Liz nodded. John was John Wilson of Wilson and Sons Funeral Home and this was a work-related call.

Gail had been employed at Wilson and Sons since 1995 when it was just Wilson's. She started there months after her husband, Liz's father, stepped up out of the subway after work, paused and then dropped to the sidewalk among the other homebound commuters, dead from a massive heart attack.

Now, though she claimed to be retired, Gail went in when John needed her—when one of his sons took time off or when someone called with a request for a painted casket; Gail painted the caskets.

"A casket?" Liz asked when her mother hung up.

"For . . . Pat Catalano."

"Pat? Your Pat? She died? How long has it been? Twenty years?"

"Shh." Gail quieted Liz. "No, she didn't die. But she must be sick. She wants to talk to me about a casket. Somehow she found out I work at Wilson's."

They sat in silence for a few moments, letting the name Pat take them back into their pasts. Liz's mind went to that summer just after her father died, when she was eleven, and she and her mother moved into the cottage on Pat's lakefront property, and then to the day they moved out and no one came to say goodbye.

Liz took a sip of wine. Gail did the same.

"I haven't thought about her in a long time," said Gail. "I wonder what made her think about me."

"If she's thinking about a coffin, maybe she remembered the birds you painted on Daddy's and she decided she wanted one like it."

Gail nodded. "Those birds made quite an impression on her."

"They made an impression on everyone."

Gail smiled wanly. "I still don't know what possessed me. Grief, I suppose."

"Daddy loved birds." Liz could remember him hushing her while they were in the park, so they could listen to a particular bird's call. And he knew birds' names. "People think that when you live in the city, you only see pigeons," he told her. "But they're not all pigeons." He taught her to distinguish the lament of the mourning dove from the coo of the pigeon. He pointed out the *thrrr* of the woodpecker and the chirp of the chickadee. He helped her spot the little crayon-yellow American goldfinch that she might otherwise have missed and that could still awe her with its scribble of color.

Her mother, in a gesture to his love of birds, decided he should have birds on his coffin. She told the director, John, that since the casket was hers, paid on credit until the life insurance came through, she had the right to do anything she wanted to it. And she wanted to paint it. John tried to talk her out of it—it just wasn't done. But he eventually gave in, and Gail painted. During the wake, people commented—the oddity of it, the beauty of the birds. They whispered about whether it was blasphemous and about the love and grief that had driven Gail to it.

Liz had not known what to think. Was it beautiful or had her mother gone crazy? But when she was required to sit in the room with her dead father in the casket, she was glad for the birds and imagined them guiding his soul to heaven.

After the wake, Wilson's Funeral Home received a few calls from people curious about the painting. Could they have birds, too? John called Gail but she and Liz had gone upstate to live with Pat. They wouldn't be back. But then they were back. And Gail went to work for John Wilson.

"I never knew what happened between us," Gail said. "We were up there that summer. I thought we were going to live there forever. And then we were back. And I never saw Pat again."

Liz watched her mother's face as she searched the past.

Later, when Liz was home, lying in bed next to her husband, she let the movie of that summer play in her memory.

After Liz's father died, Pat, Gail's best friend since high school, suggested Liz and her mother might be afraid in the city alone. Liz didn't think it was the city she was afraid of but she did know that she had become frightened. When she heard that Pat invited them to go live in the cottage on the lake, Liz was sad about leaving her friends but she wanted to be safe again. Pat and her husband, Cat, had two daughters, Carrie and Jill, and two sons, Bruce and Jimmy. Carrie was Liz's age and they had played together on previous visits, and Liz consoled herself for the loss of her school friends with this.

As soon as school let out, she and her mother moved into the guest cottage. White and cozy, the cottage was like a dollhouse to Liz, and the magic of living in it never entirely wore off.

Pat told them to treat the lake and her house, which they called The House, and which sat at the top of the lakeward-sloping property, as their own. "Come and go as you like." But Liz's mother hesitated. She worried about being presumptuous, about taking advantage and so decided that Liz shouldn't go to the lake until the other kids were there, and that neither of them should go up to The House unless they were specifically invited. On the other hand, she didn't want Liz moping around; she was to come up with a project.

Liz found drawing paper and pencils and a book titled *Trees of the Northeast* in the cottage. It came as a surprise to her that so many different species of trees existed; she had never extrapolated what her father taught her about birds to other areas of nature. She decided to learn the names of trees on the property and create a sketchbook of them. She called it, grandly, *A Study of Trees: For My Father.*

She hadn't thought of her *Study* in years, and she fell asleep wondering what had become of it.

Her mother called the next day after having talked to Pat on the phone. "She has a brain tumor. She's having surgery but she wants all her funeral arrangements made before, just in case."

"And she wants you to paint the casket?"

"Yes. She's bringing some photos. I think she wants a mural of the lake or trees from the old property. Apparently, she sold it all years ago. And it turns out that she's living just two towns away from here. She's coming over Sunday. Would you mind coming over, too? This whole thing has me rattled."

At first, Liz was afraid of the trees—there were so many clumped together by the lake and their leaves blocked the sun and created a threatening darkness. Some of the branches plunged close to the ground as if they intended to catch her by the ankles. The roots menaced her, too, bulging like thick veins on an old woman's hands. But she was committed to her project and willed herself to be brave. She let herself be drawn to a kind-looking tree with a whitish bark, and she turned the pages in her guide until she found something that resembled it—paper birch. She tried to draw it but she didn't have her mother's talent and so, she peeled a bit of the bark and picked up a fallen leaf and later taped them alongside her crude sketch for a deeper study.

She learned pin oaks and the root-beery smell of the sassafras leaf when she folded it. She ripped the skin of her knee climbing into the crux of a catalpa but climbed again and discovered that from that spot, she had an almost unobstructed view of The House and the lakefront. It quickly became her routine to scramble up to her branch and listen for the sounds from the house that carried over the placid water.

It was always the boys who flew noisily from the house first, running down the lawn and onto the dock barefoot, hurling themselves into the lake. Carrie followed, and they performed what Liz learned was a ritual imposed by Cat—the daily swim back and forth across the lake. Liz would hug her catalpa feeling left out— neither a swimmer nor a member of the rambunctious family—as the three thrashed by. But she consoled herself with an image of her skimming across the surface of the lake like a dragonfly, effort- lessly beating them all.

On the best days, Gail and Pat would sit in lounge chairs on the lawn, sometimes smoking, often sipping at drinks. There was lots of laughter—Pat's, deep and swooping, Gail's, a short burst, as though humor always caught her off guard—and Liz was buoyed by the sound. Some days, Pat would bring out paints and Gail would help her set up easels, and the two of them would paint. Later, some of the kids might join in. Jill rarely came down. Carrie and Liz often ate their sandwiches under the branches of the accommodating weeping willow—easily identified by Liz— on the front lawn. Hidden by its dangling fingers of leaves, they made it their treehouse, and that was where they told each other secrets: Liz of her fear that her mother would die, too; Carrie of Jill smoking cigarettes and sometimes pot in her bedroom. (Liz had to ask what pot was.).

Not long after they settled into the cottage, Cat began visiting Gail and Liz to make repairs on a holey screen door, a stuck drawer. He brought plastic chairs for sitting outside and citronella candles. At first, his gruffness alarmed Liz, but then he began teaching her how to fix things. He said it was important to be helpful, and he complained that his kids weren't. She found herself wanting to please him, so she paid attention when he changed a bulb, oiled the hinges on the door, changed the batteries in the flashlight and the fire alarm. He noticed her *Study of Trees* sitting on the bedstand and thumbed through it, saying it was worthwhile to take the time to learn about nature. When he asked her which was her favorite tree, she said the weeping willow, and he said it was his favorite, too: "that's our special tree." She was thrilled at what she perceived as their shared ownership of the tree. She began wandering into the garage early in the morning while the others swam where she found him working on some project. She told him about another tree she identified and watched while he replaced a belt in the car, fixed a vacuum cleaner, built something out of wood. She would stay until Carrie came looking for her. Carrie would be mystified as to what was so fascinating but also jealous enough of the attention Liz was getting to feign interest. To please Cat, Liz asked Carrie to teach her to swim. Her plan was to become good enough to beat everyone and then surprise Cat with her prowess in the water.

In bed at night, Liz fantasized about scenarios in which Cat would become her father. In one, her greatest fear came true: her mother died. But the loss was assuaged by her absorption into the Catalano family where she soon became the favored child.

When the bell rang on the Sunday of Pat's visit, Gail quickly hugged Liz, took a deep breath and went to the door. "Pat."

"Hello." It was the same husky voice Liz remembered.

Gail led her in.

"Liz? Is that you?" Pat asked.

"It is."

"Grown up, of course."

"It's good to see you," Liz said, as she took in the changes. The last time she saw her, Pat was probably close to Liz's current age of thirty-two. Now, her hair was silver, though it was cut in the same short style Liz remembered. And her sun-damaged face showed how much she had enjoyed being outdoors. She leaned on a cane.

"Yes," Gail agreed. "It's good to see you." She, too, noted the changes in Pat, and Pat seemed to be reconciling Gail's appearance—her dyed blonde hair, the extra weight—to the image of Gail she held in her head from over twenty years ago.

"Come in," Gail offered. "What a surprise it was to hear from you. Sit."

"I remembered you had gone to work at the funeral home. Your letters."

"Yes. I wrote you. You never answered."

Without addressing the issue of the unanswered letters, Pat went on. "Strangely, I remembered the name of the funeral home, and I remembered that you told me you painted coffins."

"Some special requests," Gail said.

"That all started with your birds on Frank's coffin?"

"You remember the birds? I thought you might."

"Of course. I never forgot them."

"Can I get you some coffee?"

"I'd love it. Black. I'm not supposed to have caffeine but . . . what the hell? And are you in the funeral business, too?" she asked Liz.

"No, no," Liz repudiated it with a wave of her hand. "I do landscape design." She had endured endless taunting about her mother's work, including a persistent rumor that she had once taken a boyfriend to the funeral parlor to have sex in a coffin; it was an entrenched habit to vehemently deny any association with coffins.

Pat nodded. "Yes. You and trees . . . ." She let that thought go. "But you live here with your mother?"

"No. I'm married. My husband and I live nearby."

"Oh. For some reason, I always thought of you two together."

Gail brought the coffee.

"So," Pat asked, "what have you been doing? Painting coffins. What kinds of paintings do you do?"

"Let me think. Oh, one was of a beach scene. The woman loved the beach. She died of skin cancer but her family said she wanted to go 'lying on the beach.'"

"I can certainly understand that. I was always a sun worshipper." Pat paused. "So, you know why I'm here."

Gail waited.

"I thought of calling you when Cat died, of doing something on his coffin. But to be honest, he always thought the birds were a little strange."

"Cat died?" Gail asked. "I didn't know. I'm so sorry."

"Prostate cancer. I could never get him to go to the doctor. He spent all his time at work or in the garage, or volunteering at that stupid fire station . . ."

"Safety Cat," Liz said.

Pat chuckled. "We used to call him that. Do you remember?"

"He made us all learn CPR the summer we were there," Liz recalled. She had been the most attentive student, and Cat had awarded her with a pin that said, "CPR Saves Lives," that she wore every day. In her mind, the pin was evidence that she was his favorite—an honorary daughter, maybe better than a real daughter. Carrie's jealousy of the pin was further proof of Liz's position.

"When did he die?" Gail asked.

"Oh, it's been a few years now," she said. "Eleven. Time goes by." She sipped her coffee, grimaced against its heat.

"We separated, you know."

"No, I didn't know," Gail answered.

"He moved into the cottage for a while. Then he got a place in town. But he moved back in when he got sick. I didn't want him to be alone."

"Of course not. I wish you had told me." After an uncomfortable pause, Gail said, "Pat, I never really knew what happened that summer."

"I don't know if any of us did." She looked at Liz. "I think things got exaggerated and . . . and then Jill ran away . . . and I didn't want to believe . . ."

"How is Jill?" Gail asked.

"She can't seem to get it right. She's been divorced twice. In and out of jobs. Poor kid."

Liz had never connected her mother's split with Pat with anything she had done. But now a blameful memory rushed at her.

One night in mid-August of that summer, Jill didn't come home. They had seen little of her; she worked in town, went out with friends, or kept herself locked up in her room listening to music. Cat went looking for her. Gail stayed up with Pat; Liz slept in Carrie's room. They whispered about how Jill was probably out with a boyfriend and how much trouble she'd be in when Cat found her. But in the morning, Jill wasn't back and coffee was on downstairs. While the adults made phone calls and took photos of Jill out of albums, Carrie and Liz tried to stay out of the way. They talked in Carrie's room, then made sandwiches and took them out to their treehouse.

"Jill and I used to hide from my brothers here," Carrie told Liz. "And we played cards, and she kissed her boyfriends here. And we used to have campouts. She would tell me what boys like to do with girls. When she comes back, she'll tell me everything she did while she was gone. I won't be able to tell you because it'll be just for us. Sisters have secrets. You don't know because you don't have a sister."

Liz knew that Carrie was probably lying and that Jill wouldn't take her into her confidence. She had done nothing but ignore Carrie when she was home. But Carrie persisted. "She'll want me to sleep in her room so she can tell me everything. Or we might sleep out here in sleeping bags. Then you won't be able to come here anymore because you can't hear the secrets."

Liz felt herself being pushed out of the family just when Cat had secured her spot with the CPR pin. "This is your father's favorite tree," she said. "And it's mine, too. He said it's our special tree. So, I can come here anytime I want."

"It's *my* favorite tree," Carrie argued. "And Jill's. And *ours*." She stretched the word into two syllables. "Not yours. You can't come under it if I say you can't. And he's *my* father. You don't even have a father. You don't even have a real family."

Carrie had said the thing that Liz had been made acutely aware of since moving onto the property; compared to the size and bustle of Carrie's family, Liz and her mother barely constituted one. She had nothing but her fantasies to fight back with.

"Your father said he wished I was his daughter!" Liz shouted.

"Liar!" Carrie yelled, scampering out from under the weeping willow.

Liz followed. "And we have a secret, too." Then she added something that was almost true. "We come here and I sit on his lap." She remembered sitting on her father's lap and it being the safest place in the world, and her grief and fear and longing for a father jumbled into something she could make herself see, even remember—her sitting on Cat's lap.

"He's not your father," Carrie shouted and stomped toward the house.

Later that day, police came. Rowboats pushed into the lake, and men in wetsuits jumped in while everyone waited on the lawn. They didn't find Jill, but Pat and my mother cried anyway.

Over the next couple of days, after police and Pat talked to several of Jill's friends, it was determined that she had run away. After that, everyone's fear turned to anger and there was lots of yelling and then lots of silence. The morning swims stopped; no one went in the lake again that summer. Cat didn't come down to the cottage. Carrie invited a school friend over one day later in the week and made it clear Liz was not included. Carrie and Pat made a trip to the mall and didn't ask Liz and Gail to come along. Gail told Liz they should stay out of the way, so they spent most of their time reading, drawing, playing Go Fish.

One evening, nearly two weeks after Jill left, Pat walked down to the cottage. "We got a postcard from Jill today," she said.

"Apparently, she's in Colorado with some boy." Then she told Gail it was time to start thinking about getting a place of her own.

"I blamed Cat for everything," Pat reflected. "He was always hard on the kids. I blamed him for driving Jill away." She looked at Liz. "And then Carrie told me about you and . . . the weeping willow."

Gail asked, "Told you about what?"

"About Liz and Cat. Under the weeping willow."

"What?" Gail turned to her daughter. "What about you and Cat? Did he hurt you?"

"No. Of course not."

Gail turned back to Pat. "Please, I have no idea what you're talking about."

Pat shook her head. "I should have told you but . . . I was sick at the thought. And I didn't want to believe it."

"What?"

"Carrie said that Liz told her that Cat would take her under the weeping willow . . ."

"Oh God. Oh no. Liz?"

She shifted to the edge of the couch. "Mom, calm down. Nothing happened. It wasn't like that."

"What was it?"

"I don't know." She had memories of sitting on Cat's lap. Over the years, she had conflated him with her father. But now she realized those memories were ones she couldn't trust. "I really missed Dad and I wanted a father. I wanted Cat to love me . . ." She could still feel the ache. "I remember the weeping willow and Cat being good to me. He never hurt me. Never."

"I didn't want to believe it," Pat said. "But once I had it in my head, I couldn't get rid of it. When I said something to him, he hated me for even asking." She shook her head. "We just fell apart after that. All of us."

"You should have told me," Gail said to Pat.

"I didn't know what to do. The only thing I could think of was to ask you to leave." Pat stayed in the past for a few moments, then sighed. "It was all so long ago. We made our peace when he got sick." She shook her head. "So much time lost." She looked at Gail. "I wanted to make my peace with you, too. I missed you."

"I missed you, too." Gail reached out to hold Pat's hand.

Pat took another deep breath, released her hand and patted her thighs. "So, I told you . . . there's something growing in my head."

Gail let out a long breath. Liz stared at the floor processing the destruction she had caused.

"They want to try to shrink it with chemo and radiation. And then maybe they'll do surgery. But . . . it's pretty bad. So, I want to order my box, just in case."

Gail smiled. "Your box?"

"Yes. I don't want to call it a coffin." She paused. "When I sold the property, it was full of bad memories, but now when I think of it, it calms me. There were good memories, too." She reflected, "We raised the kids there. We loved the lake and all our picnics on the lawn and campouts under the weeping willow. We found Boots, our first cat, under that tree. So, I've been thinking that I'd like to go back to some of that. Rest in that when the time comes. My own little heaven. If that doesn't sound too melodramatic."

"Not at all," Gail answered.

"So, what do we do now?" Pat asked.

"I could do a few sketches."

"Do you remember it?" Pat asked.

"Of course."

"I have a couple of photos that the realtor used." Pat took an envelope from her purse. "I can leave these with you." She moved to the edge of her chair and pushed herself up and leaned on her cane. "And now I better get going. I get tired pretty easily." She smiled. "How long do you think it will take?"

"I'll have them ready in a day or two."

"Let's hope there's not that much of a rush," Pat smiled. "It was good to see you."

"You, too." Gail and Pat hugged.

Liz walked over and hugged her, too. "I'm so sorry."

At the door, Pat said to Gail, "Make it beautiful."

Gail came back into the room and sat down. "All these years without Pat."

"Mom, I'm so sorry. I never realized what I said had anything to do with what happened between you and Pat. I loved Cat. I just wanted him to love me."

Gail interrupted. "And all these years without a father for you."

Liz sat next to her mother and leaned into her.

"We both lost so much," Gail said.

After a few minutes, Liz wiped her eyes, handed her mother a tissue, and pointed to the envelope on the coffee table. "Want to look at those?"

Gail shook her head. "No. I want to remember it the way I remember it. It can't be any more beautiful in the photos than it is in my memory."

Liz nodded. It was beautiful in her memory, too. She realized she had misunderstood the birds on her father's coffin. They weren't there to take him to heaven. The painting was meant to be heaven, a heaven of beautiful birds for him. And now her mother would paint a heaven for Pat, a beautiful heaven full of trees and sweet memories that Pat would lie down in when the time came.

TUESDAY NIGHT AT THE STOP AND SHOOT

Damian checks himself out in the locker room mirror at 9:30 p.m. Tuesday night. White jacket. White tie. White shirt and pants. "Welcome to The Shop and Shoot," he says. "Damn, I look good."

Mort kind of rolls his eyes, the way he always does with Damian. But I nod and say, "You do," because Damian does. He takes his appearance seriously and I respect that.

Damian turns and gives me kind of a hard fake punch and says, "Someday, my man. Someday, you'll wear the jacket, too."

"You know it," I say, and nod again. I'm still a Buddy and Buddies don't get to wear white jackets. When I get promoted to Master Buddy, I'll wear one. "I'm with you tonight in orientation," I tell Damian.

"Good. Watch and learn. Watch and learn."

Damian always says this, and Mort rolls his eyes again. Damian just shakes his head like there's nothing to be said or done about Mort and heads upstairs for a vanilla milkshake. He always has a shake before his shift. We're allowed two free snacks a night. Of course, the Master Buddies' list of approved snacks is more extensive than the Buddies' list. We're allowed shakes, too, but smaller ones.

"He's such an asshole," Mort says.

"Yeah, but he's good at his job," I remind Mort. I like Mort. He's funny and he's a good Buddy, but I don't think he'll ever make Master Buddy. He hasn't got the drive. I look in the mirror. I think I look good, too, but I don't say it because I don't want Mort thinking I'm an asshole, too. "Welcome to The Shop and Shoot," I say into the mirror.

"You going to practice the Guidelines again?" Mort asks. "Want me to listen?" The Guidelines are the instructions for The Shop and Shoot. Master Buddies get to take the customers into the orientation room and tell them the Guidelines. The MBs have to memorize the script and be really enthusiastic and dynamic. Damian is a genius at that.

"Nah," I decide, looking at the clock. I like being on the floor early. Upstairs, Mort and I split off—he pulled The Shop tonight and I've got The Shoot.

The Greeters have already registered the new customers, charged them for membership and taken ID photos. I direct them to one of the orientation rooms and seat them. We keep things intimate at The Shop and Shoot—thirty people to a room, max. Tonight we have twenty-three. I go back for their ID cards, which I'll hand out after they get the Guidelines.

Damian blows onto the platform like a rock star, wired and ready. "Welcome to The Shop and Shoot," he calls out, applauding. The people applaud back. It's Tuesday, the crowd's quieter than on weekends, but Damian still gets them going. "I want to release you good people into the aisles and onto the range as soon as possible, so if you'll just listen up, I'll go over some guidelines to make your time here great. Now, the most important: everyone must carry a gun."

He claps again a couple of times. "That's right. At The Shop and Shoot, everyone three and older carries a gun. Even you folks planning to head for the Shop section—" MBs never say "you women heading for the Shop section" because Mr. Watsom, our boss and the owner, thinks that might make the women feel stereotyped as shoppers.

"You may think you don't require a gun," Damian continues, "but just when you're bending down to get that Dorito thirty-pack from the bottom shelf, someone pushes right into your face, blocking your way. Or maybe when you're on line, someone jumps ahead. Wouldn't you like to . . . well, shoot that someone?" Damian smiles and nods and claps some more. "Come on, admit it," Damian says. "I want to shoot people all the time. That's why we have The Shop and Shoot."

I nod and clap to encourage folks, and they look at each other and nod, too. It's clear they're getting excited. Except this one guy, who looks unsure and won't meet anyone's eye. Sometimes people come, then think they don't really want to be here. But deep down, the guy knows why he came, just like most people know. That's the genius of this place. It gives people permission to admit what they really want.

"Now, me, personally," Damian continues, "I think The Shop's sometimes more challenging than The Shoot. Your targets are unexpected there, and you have to be alert."

Here a woman nudges her husband or boyfriend and says, "See?"

"But you shoppers, you do what you want—you can shoot all the targets that pop up or you can ignore them all and just shop. Plenty to shop for—we have it all, from cars to tomato paste. Check out Aisles One to Seventy-Two. You'll find restrooms and snack bars all along the way, and plenty of Buddies to help with whatever you need. We believe in service here. And we don't just say that; we mean it."

That's another thing I admire about Mr. Watsom. He knows people are sick and tired of snotty cashiers and serve-yourself-everything stores. He knows people want service, and he gives it to them.

"Okay," Damian continues. "So you'll all get a directory and a map. If you want to, you can stay after this part for the 3D virtual tour. Okay? Now here's how The Shoot works." People lean forward.

"When you go onto the range, they'll direct you to a booth. In there's a list of targets. Each kind of target has its name printed, along with a picture to help those of you who might not be sure what the picture means." The pictures are really for those whose English isn't so good, but we don't want to make anyone feel bad about that. We don't discriminate here at The Shop and Shoot.

"You'll also notice that the targets are color-coded. The first group is pink. Pink targets won't get you many points, but they'll give you practice. Yes, we do track points here at The Shop and Shoot. That's for your benefit, because racking up more points earns you free targets.

"The pink targets are first, and they're inanimate things, okay? Non-living. Paper targets, cans on stumps, the side of a barn, etc. You move onto blue targets, you raise your points a bit. Here you have your raccoons, birds, rats, mice—all those annoying little critters who won't stay out of your yard or who crap on your car."

Laughs and nods.

"In the brown group, you'll find dogs and cats. Now, I know you all love your pets, but you know there's been times when someone's dog tore up your yard, or barked all night, and you just wish you could—" Damian pauses here and puts out his hand, inviting the audience.

They shout back, "Shoot it!"

"Well, now's your chance. And what about your boss? Let's talk about these green targets. Haven't we all wanted to kill our bosses?"

The truth is, I'd never want to kill Mr. Watsom. I respect him too much. I give him credit, though, for knowing that people often do hate their bosses, and I admire him for not being afraid to make himself a target, so to speak.

"And now the teens, the bright orange targets. Forgive me, you teens out there, but hasn't there been a time when everyone has wanted to kill a teenager? The loud music, the bad attitudes. I know there were a few times my mother wanted to kill me."

Some of the teens boo, but they're smiling.

"On the other hand, you guys, come on—I know, believe me, I know, I was a teenager up until a year ago—haven't you wanted to kill your mother? Or your father? Go ahead, admit it! And aim for those gray targets."

Now the teens hoot and pump their fists.

"And let's hear it for husbands and boyfriends. Yeah, I know we're impossible. And— sorry, ladies—but you guys out there, don't you just want to kill them sometimes?"

Someone yells out, "Oh, yeah."

"Yeah," Damian says. "So go for the red."

Now they're all stirred up, smiling, laughing, pointing at each other, saying, "I'm going to kill you tonight!" Everyone except the quiet guy.

"Okay," Damian says. "You can choose the beige Generic Male or Generic Female, or you can get really specific and move on to the purple targets, where you choose by race or religion: Chinese, Jewish, African, Catholic, Dominican, Indian, Irish, whatever. We put Homosexual in that category, too, because, well, where else would you put it? So go for it. Express yourself!

"That about does it, except for Scenarios and Taboos. The silver and the gold. Scenarios cost a little more. Well, actually, a lot more, but believe me, they're worth it. You pick the place: park, movie theatre, train, school. We have a whole list. Your place, we load it up with people. And then—" Damian pauses for effect. "You come in and shoot to your heart's content.

"As far as the Taboos, well, I don't want to give too much away, but you folks are smart. You know what a taboo is, right?" Here, Damian shows why he's a Master Buddy. For those who don't know, but don't want to look stupid by asking, he says, "You know, something you're really not supposed to do. For example, some people say it's taboo to kill an infant. Others think it's taboo to shoot at a crucifix. See?

"Anyway, you push the big gold button under the word

Taboos and see what comes up. You have to be a little daring, I admit, because you don't know what you'll have to shoot.

"All right. Let's get out there." Damian used to ask if people had questions, but some woman almost always asked too many, which made the rest impatient. Now he skips questions and reminds people that The Shop and Shoot has Buddies and Master Buddies on the floor to answer their questions.

I hand out the IDs and tell people they have to wear them the whole time. "We like to know that everyone at The Shop and Shoot belongs here," I add. They like that. It makes them feel part of a special group, which they are, and it makes them feel safe.

Damian shoots me a look then nods toward the quiet guy. He's noticed him, too. Masterful! That's my signal to follow. Damian gives me the ones who look like they're not sure; he takes the ones who look like they'll spend big. I understand; the MB who signs up the most targets per month gets a bonus.

I get next to my guy. He's easy to track because he kind of looks like me when I'm out of uniform, but older. Jeans, blue T-shirt. Short brown hair, brown eyes. My height. "Hey, I'm Zed," I say. That's not my real name, of course; we all have floor-names.

"Luke," he replies.

"What kind of targets are you after, Luke?"

"I don't know. Generic Male, I guess," he says.

"Ever been here before?"

He shakes his head. "Nah."

"You're gonna love it." Luke doesn't answer. That's okay. I can do the talking for both of us. I walk him to his booth, push the beige Generic Male button for him. He picks up the gun, stretches out his arms, cups the heel of his left hand in his right palm—he's a leftie, like me—and settles into his aim.

He pulls the trigger and drops his arms slowly. He stares at the target a moment. He puts down the gun and pulls the cord, bringing the target close so he can see where he hit. Over the left eye.

"Great shot." I like it when my customers hit their targets. It makes them happy. "Hey, I'm a southpaw, too."

"Yeah?"

"Yeah. Do you want to go for another target?" I ask. "Some extra points? What about an animal?"

He shakes his head. "I don't want to shoot an animal."

"Sure. Okay. What about your boss? Or girlfriend?" I raise my eyebrows to encourage him; I learned that from Damian.

"Nah." He pauses. "There's no girlfriend." His eyes move around like he's embarrassed and doesn't want to look at me. And doesn't want me to look at him. So I just push the GM button again. Another target pops up, and Luke gets ready to shoot. He hits four more targets and that's it. He's done.

"Thanks," he says before he leaves.

I nod. "No problem." I think I handled him pretty well.

Luke comes in every Tuesday for the next few weeks, and he always looks for me. He never says much, but that's fine. I think he likes me because I don't ask him a lot of questions. I just let him be, and let him know he has a place here at The Shop and Shoot.

Most people tell you who they're shooting. We're not supposed to ask, it might make them self-conscious or guilty. But people like to tell. Last Friday, I got a girl in here, maybe sixteen. Right after I greeted her, she said, "I'm going to blow my boyfriend away. He's Puerto Rican and Irish. You got a target like that?" We don't, but I showed her the Puerto Rican Male and the Irish Male, and she said the Puerto Rican looked more like him than the Irish, except that he had blue eyes. She shot twenty-five PRMs.

Not Luke. He doesn't come in angry, and he doesn't say who his GM is, and he doesn't want any other target. I find something pure in the way he sticks to that one target. Another thing I like about Luke is that he's what we Buddies call a Lone Shooter. We're of two minds about them at The Shop and Shoot. Some of us like the weekend crowds, and others prefer the weekday customers. Mort and I diverge; he's a weekend man. His crowd always comes here primed, knowing what they want. And they want it all. They come in groups and on dates.

Almost no one comes alone unless they're meeting someone. Last Saturday we had a group like that, guys who shot at their targets and kept yelling to each other, "This is you, dude!" They were also BitchKillers, as we call them. You know, "Hasta la vista, bitch." We always get a bunch of those on weekends.

I prefer weekdays. People coming in then are more particular and thoughtful about their choices. Plus you get your regulars, and your Lone Shooters like Luke, so it just seems more civilized to me.

Tonight, I'm all set at his regular time—10 p.m.—and there he is.

"Hey, Luke."

"Hey."

"How's things?"

"Great."

But he doesn't sound like they're great. I think he's lonely; I just get that impression because he never comes with a friend. He's also pretty thin, so maybe he jogs. He's about thirty-five or forty, but I'm not a good judge of age. Tonight he looks even older. Dark circles under his eyes. Probably not sleeping. Maybe sad about something. I want to cheer him up.

"How about a Scenario tonight?" I feel like I have to persuade him even though I don't expect him to give in. "You could do a Generic Male Scenario. We could arrange that. Shake up the routine a little bit." I'm starting to think a change might do him good.

"No, thanks," he says.

He's always polite. I walk him to his booth and set up a GM for him. He hits just one target and puts down the gun.

"That's it?" I ask, surprised. He usually shoots at least five Generic Males.

"That's it," he says. "Bye. Thanks." He shakes my hand. He's never done that before. I've never seen anyone shoot just one target. Never. Luke stays on my mind.

After my shift, I'm allowed five targets on the range, categories pink through red—no Scenarios or Taboos until I make Master Buddy. Tonight I pull Generic Male. I want to do just the one target, like Luke, to see how it feels. After one, though, I'm just not satisfied. I hit the Generic Male button again and wonder why Luke didn't choose a race or religion.

Who does he shoot that has no race or religion? Is Luke gay, and shooting a lover who left? Still, he doesn't strike me as gay, and he never chose an HM target. I take another shot. Is it his father? Why not The Father target, then?

I set up my third target, seeing Luke the way he would set it up. Determined. Eyes narrow. Face set. Thin face. Pale. I wonder what nationality Luke is. White, yeah. Irish? Maybe. Polish? Possibly. Nothing distinguishable. Just white. I take my shot. Then it hits me. Generic Male. Luke is Generic Male.

He's shooting himself. Every week, he comes in and shoots himself.

Wow. Now I can't wait for him to come back. But I can't say anything to him. It's against all the rules to comment on a customer's choice of target, even if the target is himself. I can't risk making him feel self-conscious, making him feel like he can't come back here. Because if he can't shoot himself here, where can he shoot himself? No, I just have to be here for him.

All week, I can hardly think of anything but Luke. Tuesday finally comes, and I keep checking the time. Nine. Nine-thirty. Ten. Finally. But no Luke. Eleven. Midnight. No Luke. All night. No Luke.

Maybe he moved, I tell myself. Or got himself a girlfriend. But in my gut, I have this feeling: Luke shot himself.

It isn't my fault, but I feel kind of guilty. Like I should have done something. Like maybe he was telling me and I should have figured it out sooner. Then I think that maybe he should never have come to The Shop and Shoot in the first place, that if there was no Shop and Shoot, maybe he would never have gotten the idea to shoot himself. I don't like thinking this way.

I tell Mort about it. He sets me straight. "First off," he says, "you don't know that he's dead. He could have just moved. He could have gotten a girlfriend. Maybe he's busy getting laid."

"Maybe."

"Don't torture yourself. A guy's got to take responsibility for his own actions. You know that. You know the rules. Don't force anyone into a target they don't want. Did you force this guy?"

"No."

"Right. We suggest, but we don't force. As Mr. Watsom says, we're not doing them any favors if in the end they don't take responsibility for their own targets. Right?" I feel less guilty.

"He came in here knowing what he wanted. And he gave himself what he wanted. That's the whole point of The Shop and Shoot? Just keep doing your job and keep practicing your Guidelines." Maybe Mort understands The Shop and Shoot better than I do.

Luke stays on my mind, though, when I practice that night. I know this because I do something I've never done before. Right after I say, "The most important guideline is that everyone must carry a gun," I make my hand into a gun and point it at the mirror. At my reflection. At me. That's when the idea hits me.

My meeting with Mr. Watsom goes well. He likes the idea of a suicide target. "We might even create a High Taboo category for it," he says.

"We could use the ID photos," I say. "Blow them up and apply them to the body of any target—GM, Latin Female, whatever. Then, if a person went into the High Taboo category, up would come a target of him or her. What a rush that would be! To see your own face come up on a target. It would be the ultimate Shop and Shoot experience!"

"Great idea!" he says.

My mind works fast. "We could even have self-targets pop up

in The Shop section, maybe in dressing rooms when the things people try on don't fit."

Mr. Watsom laughs. "Brilliant!" he says, shaking my hand. "I love a Buddy who's always thinking. And clearly, you are thinking. Brush up on your Guidelines, Zed, because this idea of yours could bring us many more customers. So many we might need more Master Buddies. Be ready."

"I'll be ready Mr. Watson." I'm already rehearsing in my head: *Welcome to the Shop and Shoot.*

TAKING NOTES

"You okay?" Don called from the living room.

That was his contribution to the packing of the suitcases, a call into Deb once in a while.

"Fine."

"Bulletproof," the man on Orchard Street where they bought the luggage had boasted. Deb had narrowed her eyes. "Bulletproof," he repeated. She and Don looked at the fabric of the suitcase. They were buying luggage for their honeymoon—a week at an expensive resort in Puerto Rico. "That settles it," Don said. "We'll take it. You never know, right?'" He mocked the man without the man knowing it and later made a story of it for their friends. "If we get shot at, I might not make it, but my shirts will."

She was stuffing their underwear into the front pocket of the big suitcase when her fingers touched paper. Knowing exactly what she had discovered, she pulled out a folded piece of loose-leaf and an envelope-less card with a kitty-cat on the front. She opened it and there were the sickeningly familiar looping letters: "Don, you're the best man I know. Someone should tell you that every day and appreciate you. Love, Kathie," with the L and the K embellished with curlicues.

Deb became aware of the pulse at her temples. Thimp. Thimp. Thimp. A coldness like fear squirted into her stomach. They could still do that to her. She unfolded the loose-leaf and read hurriedly, though it was more like reciting at this point; she knew the lines so well. "Dear Don, I want you to know you have a fan; someone should tell you you're such a good man. You're thoughtful and kind; you're such a good find . . ." She skimmed the couplets to the closing which was an "I Love You, Kathie," with the same exaggerated script.

Deb sat on the bed amid the aqua- and coral-colored summer clothes, and pressed her temples, a note in each hand.

"Did you call me?" Don inquired from the doorway.

Startled, Deb shoved the notes back into the suitcase pocket as if it were she who were guilty of something.

"You okay?" Don asked when she didn't answer.

Deb picked up a shirt and laid it in the suitcase. She placed three more in without seeing any of them.

"You mad? What did I do?"

"You know what you did."

"What?"

She continued to put clothing into the bulletproof suitcase, took a deep breath, and another, let a few moments pass, exhaled through pursed lips, which helped her control her heartbeat and dissipate her rage. She and Don were leaving for Arizona—Phoenix and Sedona—the next morning, and she didn't want the trip ruined.

Who goes to the desert in July? Don had asked, reducing all her planning to a joke. He asked it every time she told anyone where they were going on vacation. *Who goes to the desert in July?* But she was a teacher, and July and August were the only months she could travel, and Don knew that and he really didn't mean to hurt her by mocking her choice; he just couldn't let the opportunity to say something funny go by. And he did make her laugh no matter how much she didn't want to. But desert or not, she wanted to enjoy this trip; they could fight when they came back. Until then, she could pretend she hadn't found the letters; she could pretend, again, that she had thrown them out, as she promised she would.

"Did you want me to help you?" Don asked, coming and standing over the bed as though he might really assist her. "Is that what you're mad about?"

Without looking at him, she asked, "Do we have Advil?"

"You have a headache?"

"I'm getting one." Her voice quavered. "Actually, I need some ginger ale. I'm a little nauseous."

"Are you getting sick?"

She flicked her eyes up to him and then back down. "Can you just get me some ginger ale?"

"Okay. I'm going."

Later when he suggested a "little pre-vacation fooling around," she said, "If you get on top of me, I'll vomit on you."

"More ginger ale?" he asked.

The first time she found the notes, she was alone packing for their trip to California. They were flying to San Francisco, renting a car and driving down Route 1 to LA. If he had been home, she might have confronted him immediately and angrily. But by the time he got back from work, she decided to wait. She told herself that the notes were probably harmless; that they could be ancient history, mementos from a past relationship that had somehow made their way into the suitcase. She didn't believe Don would cheat on her. And she wanted to see California. She thought she could pretend she never saw them. Yet, she replaced them in the pocket of the suitcase, deciding to bring them along, knowing that taking them meant she'd bring them up at some point. And as it turned out, she couldn't wait long. On the plane, after a Bloody Mary, she asked bluntly, "Would you ever have an affair?" Before he could decide what he'd say, she quoted, "'I want you to know, you have a fan; someone should tell you you're such a good man.'" He looked confused. "Kathie," she reminded him. "The poet? Kathie with an I-E." He said he didn't know what she was talking about. She told him there were love letters in the front pocket of their suitcase from someone named K-a-t-h-i-e. A flash of recognition crossed his face. "Tell me," she demanded.

"I never looked at the letters. She gave them to me and I stuffed them in the suitcase and forgot all about them."

"Who?" Deb learned that two women from the office, one named Kathie, had joined him and several other coworkers on what was supposed to be a guys golf weekend. Deb had heard about their shenanigans—so drunk at dinner, they were asked to leave the restaurant; so drunk on the golf course, one of them bellyflopped into the water to retrieve a ball. She hadn't heard about the women.

She didn't believe he had cheated. He wouldn't do that to her. He was annoying but he was loyal. He might flirt but that would be as far as he'd go. This Kathie probably was infatuated with him; everyone loved Don. Still, she wanted him to suffer a bit, so she pressed.

Then he told her. He was really drunk; she was really drunk. It never happened again, would never happen again. He vaguely remembered her giving him the notes at the airport; he must have slipped them into the suitcase and forgotten about them.

Deb thought about leaving him. She made him get tested for HIV. When she would have sex with him again, she made him wear condoms. At the nine-month mark, she worried about Kathie presenting him with a baby or with child support demands and that reminded her of her anger. She was reminded again, when, a year and a half after the incident, she was packing for their trip to Montreal and she found the notes again. The second time was no easier than the first. But she promised herself she wouldn't bring it up again, but then there she was, half-drunk on red wine, reciting the poem. He had looked at her as though he didn't know what she was talking about. "Kathie. Kathie of the poems." She hated him all over again, not just for fucking Kathie but because that poem was burned in her memory and he had never bothered to read it.

On the plane, seated at the window, she envisioned a string of elastic being pulled tauter and tauter as the plane lifted. At some point during this visualization, she wanted the elastic to snap, separating her from everything below, allowing her to leave it all behind—her worries about the next class of third-graders she'd get in September, her aging parents, the repairs their house needed, their arguments. His cheating. When it snapped, it would all be down there and she'd be up in the air, rising away from it. But she couldn't make it snap. The plane pulled and the string pulled. But no snap.

Don leaned in to share her view. He gently elbowed her, saying, "Cheer up. It's vaa-cation."

She couldn't help smiling. "You're such a jerk."

"But I'm your jerk." He rested his almost full head of auburn hair on her shoulder, the hair that had caught her attention and attracted her to him the first time she saw him on the baseball field of their college. Her heart still sped a little at the sight of him from a distance. She kissed the top of his head.

Dry heat or not, at 114 degrees, Phoenix was too hot. As they walked to the parking lot for their rented car, Deb beat Don to the punch. "Who goes to the desert in July?"

Two enormous, caged parrots greeted them in the cavernous lobby of the hotel. It was a relief to find the air-conditioner in the room set to sixty-eight degrees, and they stayed there for an hour, Don watching TV and Deb putting clothes in drawers.

That night they got drunk on Piña Coladas and were daring themselves to make love on the golf course when a line of one of the couplets popped into Deb's head and out of her mouth: "'Someone should tell you you're such a good man.'"

"What?" Don was still smiling impishly.

But Deb's mood quickly soured as did her stomach. She made it upstairs to the bathroom in their room before she vomited.

They cut their time in Phoenix short. But that was not unusual for them. Curtailing vacations was a routine that began on their honeymoon. Then, they were booked in a resort in Aruba for nine nights. After five days, Don mentioned the charity baseball game he'd wanted to play in at home. Bored with the beach and the casino, Deb decided to give him a wedding present. She called the airline and changed their flight, cutting three nights off their honeymoon and allowing him to get back for the game. As a thank-you, Don bought her a diamond bracelet in the jewelry store in the hotel, and that became a pattern—ending their vacations early and with jewelry.

"I don't like vacations. I feel like I'm acting when I'm on a trip." Don once justified their early exit as their plane tilted away from their vacation spot and toward home. "Do you know what I mean?"

She did know what he meant. On vacation when it was just the two of them, they seemed to always try to be a couple, doing the things they thought couples would do on vacations. At home, with work, errands, chores, and TV they seemed like a couple. And when they were out with friends laughing at and complaining about each other, they were comfortable as a couple. But on vacation, they were more like two people acting as though intimacy were comfortable. Still, Deb wanted to travel, or rather, she felt that traveling was something couples should do. So she kept planning trips.

The drive to Sedona was challenging, all snaking roads through the Coconino National Forest, hairpin turns, and hills that seemed never to crest. Twice, in anticipation of a crash, Deb sucked in her breath so noisily that Don snapped at her that she was making him nervous. She tried to distract herself with the trees.

"Ponderosa Pine," she remarked.

"Did you get that from the guidebook?" Don asked in a tone that suggested that repeating anything she read in the guidebook was somehow cheating.

"Afraid you'll learn something?" she sniped.

And then they came around a curve, and the earth turned red.

"It's otherworldly," Deb enthused, employing another description from the guidebook and fully expecting Don to mock her for it.

Instead, he agreed. "Like Mars, or something."

"I told you it'd be beautiful," she reminded him. She spoke animatedly for the rest of the drive, and when they found their motel, she suggested they drop their luggage off and go exploring right away. Don would have preferred to switch on the TV and lie on the bed for a while but he let himself be persuaded.

Wandering down the main street—Sedona was all galleries, jewelry, tarot cards and crystal shops—Deb spotted a sign for ANCIENT SITES JEEP TOURS. "Let's do it."

"I'm hungry," Don objected. "And we don't have to do everything on the first day, you know."

"By tomorrow, you'll be looking for a golf course," she predicted. She walked into the office and discovered that the next tour left in half an hour. "Enough time for you to eat something."

More than enough time, as it turned out. It was over an hour before Deb and Don climbed into a jeep. Back in the tour office, Don had been whispering, not so quietly, to Deb about how they were kept waiting, about how they could have sat down to a real lunch and a beer instead of taking tacos out and eating them as they walked. The manager explained that one of the jeeps had broken down, and he had had to send Deb's and Don's jeep to bring the people back. He kept promising, "Just a couple of minutes, now."

Deb's enthusiasm dampened, too. "But we've waited this long," she said.

When their jeep finally returned and the passengers—a couple Deb guessed was on their honeymoon—had finished thanking the guide, Deb climbed up in front and Don got in the back. The guide introduced herself as Lohanna, and Deb immediately decided it was a made-up name. When Lohanna leaned forward to shift gears, one of her small breasts became clearly visible through the oversized armhole of her shirt. She was a painter, she told them. Artistic people were drawn to Sedona because it had a way of awakening creativity. "There are places in these mountains," she said, "where the earth's energy can be felt."

"Vortexes," Deb said. "I read about them in the guidebook."

"I'll show you one."

Don leaned up from the back to give Deb's shoulder a squeeze. She knew what he was thinking. One night, while she was still planning the trip and looking through the guidebook, she told Don about the vortexes. As she expected, he played obtuse. "The earth's energy?" he asked. "You stand there, and what happens? A breeze blows up your pants? Really? How do you know it's the earth's energy and not a breeze? And isn't a breeze the earth's energy?" The more she tried to explain, the more unlikely vortexes sounded, so she couldn't help laughing with him. The vortexes became divortexes. "Places where wives take their husbands to divorce them." She laughed at that, too.

But now she didn't want to laugh; she wanted to believe in the vortexes and the 'divorotex' jokes didn't seem so funny now. Deb leaned away from him, away from his cynicism, toward Lohanna with her peekaboo breast, her veiny hands that maneuvered the jeep so confidently, and her belief in the earth's energy.

Lohanna was saying that it was limestone, mud, and sandstone that created the terra cotta color of Sedona. "The color enhances creative thinking."

Deb looked out at the landscape. Seeing red, she thought, and now, just that fast, she was seeing it literally and figuratively. *Someone should tell you you're such a good man.* She wished she could get those stupid rhymes out of her head but she couldn't. When she glanced back at Don, his head was tilted slightly to enhance his view into the armhole of Lohanna's shirt. He raised his eyes to meet Deb's and smiled, caught.

They got out of the jeep at a spot where Lohanna said a cliff-dwelling people had lived, and they hiked up to the shallow cave dwellings. Lohanna slid her hand along a rock wall. "Sometimes you can feel the energy of the people who lived here. Once I got an image of a little boy. Other people say they hear things. Singing. Chanting. I've never heard anything but every time I come up, I listen."

When Deb put her hand against the wall, Don made a sound behind her. "Woo-ouu."

"You're such an asshole."

Lohanna laughed.

"See, she thought it was funny." He cupped Deb's shoulder; she shrugged him off again.

"Let me show you the vortexes," Lohanna suggested.

"Go ahead," Deb shooed him off with a wave of her hand. "I'll catch up."

"Come on," Don urged. "Di–," he whispered the first syllable "vortex."

"Go."

When he and Lohanna had walked off, and Deb was sure Don wasn't watching, she put her hand back on the rock wall and closed her eyes. She wanted it to tell her something—something about forgiveness, which she couldn't fully embrace, something about how to stop punishing him and herself, that it was okay to love him even though he had betrayed her, that loving him didn't mean she was betraying herself.

"Deb," Don called from a short distance.

She palmed the wall one last time, but it didn't instruct her, so she gave up on it and walked toward him.

"The vortex. It's unbelievable. I really felt something."

"What, divorced?"

"No. Seriously. Come on. Lohanna showed me. You stand on this spot, and it's amazing. You really feel something."

"A breeze up your shorts?"

"No. I know I didn't believe it but it's amazing. It feels like energy or something. Like a rush." He hurried her over to an unremarkable spot where Lohanna was waiting. "Stand here." He stood there first to demonstrate, dancing his shoulders. "I got a tingle. It's incredible," he said to Lohanna.

Then he positioned Deb. She stood reverently, closed her eyes, breathed deeply. Felt nothing. "Here?" she asked.

"Right there. You don't feel anything?"

She moved around a little, made a few adjustments. Waited. "How long should it take?"

"You don't feel anything? I felt it right away. I can't believe you don't feel it. I thought you'd be the one to feel it." He looked at Lohanna again. "I can't believe she doesn't feel anything."

"Not everyone does."

Deb glared at the two of them. "Not everyone does," echoed in her head. But he and Lohanna do, she thought. She closed her eyes. Took a deep breath. She was hungry, she realized. That one taco she'd eaten wasn't enough. And she forgot to put on sunscreen and could feel the sun targeting her shoulders. She took another audible breath trying to clear her mind, deciding that the earth wouldn't speak to her if she were thinking about such mundane things as SPF. She focused attention on her feet. Was that something she was feeling there? Just an ant, which had made its way onto her sandals and was traversing her big toe. She stamped her foot to shake it off.

"Do you feel it?" Don asked hopefully.

"No." Oh, but she did feel something. "'I want you to know,'" she said with her eyes fixed on Don, "'You have a fan.'" She paused while Lohanna and Don looked quizzically at her. "'Someone should tell you you're such a good man.'"

Lohanna looked from Deb to Don and back to Deb. "Is the earth speaking to you?"

"'You're thoughtful and kind and always on my mind.'"

"Oh my God." Don turned away from her, then back.

"'You deserve only good things, and all the happiness that real love brings.'"

"Deb . . ."

"I can't believe you did that to me. To us."

Don puffed air from one cheek to the other, glanced away.

Lohanna, slowly coming to some kind of understanding, excused herself, "I'll be over by the jeep."

"It was nothing. I thought this was all over."

"You fucked her!"

"Two years ago."

"Have you been with her since?"

"No."

"Why should I believe you?"

"She got married."

"So what? You were married."

"I don't understand why you're bringing this up, why you want to ruin our vacation." He shook his head and shrugged. "I don't know what I can do." He looked at her, waiting for an answer. "Oh my God," he said. "You kept the notes, didn't you? They're still in the suitcase, aren't they?" He grabbed at his hair with both hands. "You have to let this go. You have to let this go or let me go. We can't keep doing this."

Deb felt the energy go out of her, as if the vortex was feeding on her, sucking the life out of her. "I want to go home."

Lohanna spoke a little on the jeep ride back but neither Deb nor Don responded. Deb peeked at Lohanna's breast. Actually, she wasn't peeking. She was simply looking in Lohanna's direction, and there it was presenting itself, demanding attention. Deb thought that maybe she'd complain about it to the manager. For the rest of the ride, she watched herself in the side view mirror as though she might do something to surprise herself. She noted the distance growing between her and the mountains, the storm clouds that seemed to be catching up to them.

Back in town, Don tipped Lohanna, and Deb heard him mumble an apology. Then when Lohanna was gone, he turned to Deb. "I'm sorry. I fucked up. But we can't keep doing this."

"I want to go home," Deb repeated.

On the way back to the motel, he stopped and bought a six-pack at a convenience store, and once they were back in the room, they each took a beer and went out to sit on the small terrace.

"There's a storm coming," he said, looking at the sky. And then he asked, "Are you hungry?"

He went out and got them hamburgers and while he was gone, she called the airlines and changed their flight. It cost $100 per ticket for the change.

When he came back, he took a small box out of his shorts pocket, handed it to her and said again, "I'm sorry."

She opened it. Emerald earrings.

"Your favorite," he reminded her.

She nodded.

"Please tear those letters up. Promise me."

She thought of them in the pocket of the suitcase.

"I'm glad we're going home," Don continued. "No more vacations for us."

After a while, Deb asked quietly, "What about Ireland? I thought you wanted to go to Ireland."

Don studied her.

He looked so sad and tired that if he'd stayed quiet for a moment longer, she would have succumbed and gone into the room and taken the letters from the suitcase and handed them to him to tear up.

"Ireland?" he asked in a fake brogue, breaking the spell.

So, the notes would stay right where they were, for now. *Someone should tell you you're such a good man.* "It's not the desert, though," she said. "You won't be able to make fun of us for going to Ireland in July."

"That's true." He smiled, and as though he thought he were finally forgiven, he hugged her. Then they stood at the railing of the terrace watching the family in the pool below, watching the sky for the next flash of lightning.

ABOUT THE AUTHOR

Joann Smith has published stories in many literary journals. Her work has been anthologized and selected as notable stories of the year by *Best American Short Stories*. She is also the author of *When I Was Boudicca*, a novel of historical fiction. Currently, she teaches at the Writing Institute at Sarah Lawrence College. She lives and writes in the Bronx and is most drawn to characters who find the extraordinary in their ordinary lives.